Analogies in the Holy Qur'an

Ibn Qayyim Al-Jawziyya

Translated & Comments by Al Reshah

Alreshah.net

Canada

Alreshah
www.Alreshah.net

Publisher's Note: This is translation of book without change of meaning as best as the translator could achieve with few comments in the footnote to clarify If any error is found please contact us through our website alreshah.net.

Book Layout © 2017 BookDesignTemplates.com

Analogies in the Holy Qur'an / Ibn Qayyim Al-Jawziyya. -- 1st ed.
ISBN 978-0-9936697-9-8

The Book is Index based on the verses explained, so every chapter reflects the Verse Number and Chapter number to ease access to researchers

Thanks for:
Stacey Con
Dawn Birdsong Vadbunker
Fox Buck

For their input and review of this Translation

Footnotes: Mohammad Ahmad

Contents

Al-Baqara 2:20-17

All praise is due to Allah, the Lord of the worlds. May blessings and peace be upon the best of creatures, Muhammad, and all his family and companions. Our Sheikh (may Allah have mercy on his soul) said:

Many analogies are mentioned in the Holy Qur'an, and these Qur'anic analogies are only understood by those with knowledge. An analogy means drawing a similarity between two objects in effect, approximating the intelligible to the perceivable or one tangible object to another, and considering one of them through the other. One example is what Allah (the Almighty) said about the hypocrites:

{مَثَلُهُمْ كَمَثَلِ الَّذِي اسْتَوْقَدَ نَارًا فَلَمَّا أَضَاءَتْ مَا حَوْلَهُ ذَهَبَ اللهُ بِنُورِهِمْ وَتَرَكَهُمْ فِي ظُلُمَاتٍ لَا يُبْصِرُونَ} {صُمٌّ بُكْمٌ عُمْيٌ فَهُمْ لَا يَرْجِعُونَ} {أَوْ كَصَيِّبٍ مِنَ السَّمَاءِ فِيهِ ظُلُمَاتٌ وَرَعْدٌ وَبَرْقٌ يَجْعَلُونَ أَصَابِعَهُمْ فِي آذَانِهِمْ ...} إلى قوله {... إِنَّ اللهَ عَلَى كُلِّ شَيْءٍ قَدِيرٌ} [البقرة:17-20]

{Their similitude is that of one who kindled a fire, but when it illuminated what was around him, Allah took away their light and left them in darkness [so] they could not see.} {Deaf, dumb and blind - so they will not return [to the right path].} {Or [it is] like a rainstorm from the sky within which is darkness, thunder and lightning. They put their fingers in their ears against the thunderclaps ...} until His saying {... Indeed; Allah is over all things competent.} [2:17-20].

Therefore, He set for hypocrites, based on their state, two examples: one of fire and other of water, because of what the fire and water contain of illumination, brightness and life; fire is the essence of light and water is the essence of life. Allah (the Almighty) put into the revelation that is sent down from heavens life and illumination for the hearts, which is why He called it 'an inspiration' and 'a light' and made those who accept it alive in the light, and those who reject it dead in the darkness. He informed about the hypocrites concerning their share of the revelation that they are like someone who lit a fire to illuminate around him and benefit him, and that is because they entered Islam, and were therefore enlightened, benefitted by it, believed in it and intermingled with the Muslims. However, since they had no share of the Islam's light in their hearts, it dominated them, and Allah took away their light, and He did not say 'their fire', because the fire contains illumination and scorching, so Allah took its illumination, kept for them its scorching and left them in darkness unable to see. This is the state of those who see and then close their eyes, who know and then deny, who enter

Islam then leave it with their hearts and never return to it, which is why He said {so they will not return}.

Then He mentioned their state regarding the example of water, as he compared them to people who experienced a rainstorm, which contained darkness, lightning and thunder. Thus, due to the weakness of their insight and intellect, the Qur'anic reproaching, threatening, menacing, commanding and forbidding, which resemble thunderbolts, became too intense for them. They became like someone who was exposed to a rainstorm containing darkness, lightning and thunder, so due to his weakness and fear, he placed his fingers in his ears for fear of a thunderbolt striking him. We and others have seen a lot of the Jahmi[1] Al Mubtadi'[2] wimps who, upon hearing the Qur'anic verses and Hadiths about the Divine attributes that contradict their inventions[3], turn away from them, as if they were alarmed zebras fleeing from a lion. Their wimp would say, "Close this door before us and recite something else." You see their hearts running away heedlessly.

---

[1] The term 'Jahmi' refers to the followers of Jahm ibn Safwan, who believe in determinism and that man has no free will & God don't have attributes.

[2] The term 'Mubtadi'' literally means 'innovator' or 'inventor', and it refers to people who introduce into the religion something that has no basis in the Qur'an or the Sunnah.

[3] The Messenger of Allah (ﷺ) said, "He who innovates something in this matter of ours (i.e., Islam) that is not of it will have it rejected (by Allah)." [Bukhari & Muslim]

Similarly, the polytheists, different as they are, when the monotheism is presented to them and its verses that abolish their disbelief are recited before them, their hearts shrink with aversion and they cannot bear to hear them; were they to find a way to plug their ears, they would do so. We also find the enemies of the Prophet's (PBUH) companions, when they hear the words of praise for the rightly guided Caliphs and the Companions of the Messenger (PBUH), they cannot bear that, and their hearts deny it. All of this contains a manifest similarity and an evident resemblance to their hypocrite brethren in the analogy of water given by Allah, because when their hearts were alike, their deeds were also alike.

CHAPTER 2

Ar-Ra'd 13:17

Allah (the Almighty) has stated the two analogies–the analogy of water and the analogy of fire–in Surat Al-Ra'd[4] . Allah (the Almighty) said:

{أَنْزَلَ مِنَ السَّمَاءِ مَاءً فَسَالَتْ أَوْدِيَةٌ بِقَدَرِهَا فَاحْتَمَلَ السَّيْلُ زَبَدًا رَابِيًا وَمِمَّا يُوقِدُونَ عَلَيْهِ فِي النَّارِ ابْتِغَاءَ حِلْيَةٍ أَوْ مَتَاعٍ زَبَدٌ مِثْلُهُ كَذَلِكَ يَضْرِبُ اللَّهُ الْحَقَّ وَالْبَاطِلَ فَأَمَّا الزَّبَدُ فَيَذْهَبُ جُفَاءً وَأَمَّا مَا يَنْفَعُ النَّاسَ فَيَمْكُثُ فِي الْأَرْضِ كَذَلِكَ يَضْرِبُ اللَّهُ الْأَمْثَالَ}
[الرعد:17]

{He sends down from the sky, rain, and valleys flow according to their capacity, and the torrent carries a rising foam. And from that [ore] which they heat in the fire, desiring adornments and utensils, is a foam like it. Thus, Allah presents [the example of] truth and falsehood. As for the foam, it vanishes, [being] cast off; but as for that which

---

[4] The 13th Chapter of the Holy Qur'an.

benefits the people, it remains on the earth. Thus, does Allah present examples.} [13:17]

Allah (the Almighty) likened the revelation, which He sent down for the life of the hearts, hearings and sights, to the water which he sent down for the life of the plants, and he likened the hearts to the valleys; a big heart that has room for great knowledge is like a big valley which accommodates a lot of water, and a small heart can only take up based on its capacity, like the small valley. Therefore, valleys flow according to their capacity, and hearts accommodate of guidance and knowledge according to their capacity. Just as when the torrent encounters the earth and passes by it, it carries foam and scum, similarly, when the guidance and knowledge encounter the hearts, they stir up the desires and doubts therein to remove and uproot them. This is like the medicine that stirs up, upon taking it, the body's impurities, distressing its drinker, while this is the proper effect of the medicine, because it stirs up these impurities to take them away; it does not coexist or go along with them.

Then He stated the analogy of fire, so he said {And from that [ore] which they heat in the fire, desiring adornments and utensils, is a foam like it}, meaning the scum that is produced when casting gold, silver, copper and iron, which the fire extracts, distinguishes and separates from the useful core, in order to be thrown away, discarded and cast off. The desires and doubts are similarly cast off and discarded by the believer's heart, like the torrent and the fire cast off this foam and scum, and in the bottom of the valley rests the clear and pure water, from which the people drink, irrigate their plants and give their cattle to drink. Similarly, in the bottom of the heart rests the clear and pure faith, which benefits its owner and others as well. Whoever does not understand these two analogies, does not ponder over them and does not realize the intent behind them is not worthy of them. Success is from Allah.

CHAPTER 3

Yunus 10:24

One more example is Allah's saying:

{إِنَّمَا مَثَلُ الْحَيَاةِ الدُّنْيَا كَمَاءٍ أَنْزَلْنَاهُ مِنَ السَّمَاءِ فَاخْتَلَط بِهِ نَبَاتُ الأَرْضِ مِمَّا يَأْكُلُ النَّاسُ وَالأَنْعَامُ حَتَّى إِذَا أَخَذَتِ الأَرْضُ زُخْرُفَهَا وَازَّيَّنَتْ وَظَنَّ أَهْلُهَا أَنَّهُمْ قَادِرُونَ عَلَيْهَا أَتَاهَا أَمْرُنَا لَيْلاً أَوْ نَهَارًا فَجَعَلْنَاهَا حَصِيدًا كَأَنْ لَمْ تَغْنَ بِالأَمْسِ كَذَلِكَ نُفَصِّلُ الآيَاتِ لِقَوْمٍ يَتَفَكَّرُونَ} [يونس:24]

{The example of [this] worldly life is but like rain which We have sent down from the sky that the plants of the earth absorb - [those] from which men and livestock eat - until, when the earth has taken on its adornment and is beautified and its people suppose that they have capability over it, there comes to it Our command by night or by day, and We make it as a harvest, as if it had not flourished yesterday. Thus, do We explain in detail the signs for a people who give thought.} [10:24]

He (the Exalted) compared the worldly life, which beautifies itself in the observer's eye and appeals to him and charms him with its adornment, so he leans towards it and grows fond of it under its allurement, then, when he thinks he owns it and capable over it, he is deprived of it suddenly, when he is in dire need of it, and a barrier is placed between them. He compared it to the land upon which rain falls, so it grows green, its plants flourish and its landscape becomes pleasant to behold, thus he is fooled by it and thinks he is capable of it and an owner of it, then Allah's command comes to it, and a blight suddenly strikes it, so it becomes as if it were not before, he becomes therefore disappointed and empty handed. Such is the state of the worldly life and those reliant on it, and this is a most eloquent analogy and assimilation. Since the worldly life is subjected to these blights, and Paradise is free therefrom, Allah (the Almighty) said, {وَاللَّهُ يَدْعُو إِلَى دَارِ السَّلَامِ} {And Allah invites to the Home of Peace} [10:25], and He called it here 'the Home of Peace' due to its freedom from such blights present in the worldly life. Thus, He invited all to it and he restricted guidance to whom He willed; such is His justice, and such is His bounty.

Hud 11:24

Another analogy is Allah's saying:

{مَثَلُ الْفَرِيقَيْنِ كَالأَعْمَى وَالأَصَمِّ وَالْبَصِيرِ وَالسَّمِيعِ هَلْ يَسْتَوِيَانِ مَثَلاً أَفَلا تَذَكَّرُونَ}
[هود:24]

{The example of the two parties is like the blind and deaf, and the seeing and hearing. Are they equal in comparison? Then, will you not remember?} [11:24]

Allah (The Exalted, the Almighty) mentioned the disbelievers and described that {They were not able to hear, nor did they see}, then he mentioned the believers and described that they have believed, done righteous deeds and humbled themselves to their Lord. Attributing to them the apparent and unapparent submission made one party like the blind and deaf since their hearts were blinded from seeing the Truth and deaf from hearing it, so they were compared to someone whose sight was unable to see the truest of things and his hearing was incapable of hearing voices, and the other party is of a seeing and hearing heart, like the one who sees with his eyes and hears with his ears. Thus, the verse contained two analogies and comparisons for each party, then denying the equivalence of the two parties by His saying, {Are they equal in comparison?}[5]

---

[5] The Holy Quran 11:11

Al Ankabut 29:41

Another example is Allah's saying:

{مَثَلُ الَّذِينَ اتَّخَذُوا مِنْ دُونِ اللَّهِ أَوْلِيَاءَ كَمَثَلِ الْعَنْكَبُوتِ اتَّخَذَتْ بَيْتًا وَإِنَّ أَوْهَنَ الْبُيُوتِ لَبَيْتُ الْعَنْكَبُوتِ لَوْ كَانُوا يَعْلَمُونَ} [العنكبوت:41]

{The example of those who take allies other than Allah is like that of the spider who takes a home. And indeed, the weakest of homes is the home of the spider, if they only knew.} [29:41]

He (the Exalted) mentioned that they are weak, and that those they took as allies are weaker than they are. Therefore, they are, in their weakness and the weakness of their allies, like the spider that took a home that is the weakest of homes. Based on this analogy, those polytheists are as weak as can be, because they took allies other than Allah, so they did not benefit, from these allies, except an increase in weakness, as He (the Almighty) said:

{وَاتَّخَذُوا مِنْ دُونِ اللّٰهِ آلِهَةً لِيَكُونُوا لَهُمْ عِزًّا} {كَلَّا سَيَكْفُرُونَ بِعِبَادَتِهِمْ وَيَكُونُونَ عَلَيْهِمْ ضِدًّا} [مريم:81-82]

{And they have taken besides Allah [false] deities that they would be for them [a source of] honor.} {No! Those "gods" will deny their worship of them and will be against them opponents [on the Day of Judgement].} [19:81-82]

And He (the Almighty) said:

{وَاتَّخَذُوا مِنْ دُونِ اللّٰهِ آلِهَةً لَعَلَّهُمْ يُنْصَرُونَ} {لَا يَسْتَطِيعُونَ نَصْرَهُمْ وَهُمْ لَهُمْ جُنْدٌ مُحْضَرُونَ} [يس:74-75]

{But they have taken besides Allah [false] deities that perhaps they would be helped.} {They are not able to help them, and they [themselves] are for them soldiers in attendance.} [36:74-75]

He also said, after mentioning the destruction of the polytheist nations:

{وَمَا ظَلَمْنَاهُمْ وَلَكِنْ ظَلَمُوا أَنْفُسَهُمْ فَمَا أَغْنَتْ عَنْهُمْ آلِهَتُهُمُ الَّتِي يَدْعُونَ مِنْ دُونِ اللّٰهِ مِنْ شَيْءٍ لَمَّا جَاءَ أَمْرُ رَبِّكَ وَمَا زَادُوهُمْ غَيْرَ تَتْبِيبٍ} [هود:101]

{And We did not wrong them, but they wronged themselves. And they were not availed at all by their gods which they invoked other than Allah when there came the command of your Lord. And they did not increase them in other than ruin.} [11:101]

These are four locations in the Holy Qur'an indicating that whoever takes an ally other than Allah for support, reinforcement and aid, will not gain except the opposite of his goal. The Qur'an contains more in that regard and this is among the best and most indicative analogies for the falsehood of polytheism, the loss of its people and their attainment of the opposite of their goals. If it was said, "They know that the spiders homes are the weakest of homes, so how did He deny their knowledge by His saying {if they only knew}?" The answer is that He did not deny their knowledge of the spider home's weakness, He rather denied their knowledge that seeking allies other than Him is like the spider taking a home. Had they known that, they would not have done it, but they thought that seeking allies other than Him will benefit them with honor and strength, but it turned out differently

CHAPTER 6

An-Nur 24:39-40

Another analogy is Allah's (the Almighty) saying:

﴿وَالَّذِينَ كَفَرُوا أَعْمَالُهُمْ كَسَرَابٍ بِقِيعَةٍ يَحْسَبُهُ الظَّمْآنُ مَاءً حَتَّى إِذَا جَاءَهُ لَمْ يَجِدْهُ شَيْئًا وَوَجَدَ اللَّهَ عِنْدَهُ فَوَقاهُ حِسَابَهُ وَاللَّهُ سَرِيعُ الْحِسَابِ﴾ ﴿أَوْ كَظُلُمَاتٍ فِي بَحْرٍ لُجِّيٍّ يَغْشَاهُ مَوْجٌ مِنْ فَوْقِهِ مَوْجٌ مِنْ فَوْقِهِ سَحَابٌ ظُلُمَاتٌ بَعْضُهَا فَوْقَ بَعْضٍ إِذَا أَخْرَجَ يَدَهُ لَمْ يَكَدْ يَرَاهَا وَمَنْ لَمْ يَجْعَلِ اللَّهُ لَهُ نُورًا فَمَا لَهُ مِنْ نُورٍ﴾ [النور:39-40]

{But those who disbelieved - their deeds are like a mirage in a lowland which a thirsty one thinks is water until, when he comes to it, he finds it is nothing but finds Allah before Him, and He will pay him in full his due; and Allah is swift in account.} {Or [they are] like darkness's within an unfathomable sea which is covered by waves, upon which are waves, over which are clouds - darkness's, some of them upon others. When one puts out his hand [therein], he can hardly see it. And he to whom Allah has not granted light - for him there is no light.} [24:39-40]

He (the Exalted) stated two analogies for the disbelievers: an analogy with a mirage and an analog with stacked darkness's. This is because those who turn away from guidance and truth are of two types: one type who thinks he is standing on something, but he discovers otherwise upon the exposure of the facts. Such is the state of the people of ignorance, invention and whims, who think they are upon guidance and knowledge, but when the facts are revealed, they realize that they are not standing on anything, and that their beliefs and the deeds based on them are like a mirage, which looks like water to the observer but is not real. Such are the deeds performed for someone other than Allah (the Exalted, the Majestic) or not according to His command; their performer beliefs them beneficial to him, but they are not. These are the deeds regarding which Allah (the Exalted, the Majestic) said:

{وَقَدِمْنَا إِلَى مَا عَمِلُوا مِنْ عَمَلٍ فَجَعَلْنَاهُ هَبَاءً مَنْثُورًا} [الفرقان:23]

{And We will regard what they have done of deeds and make them as dust dispersed.} [25:23]

Observe as Allah made the mirage in a lowland, which is the deserted land devoid of buildings, trees, plants and people. Thus, the mirage is in a deserted land with nothing therein, and the mirage itself is not real, which conforms to their deeds and hearts that have become devoid of faith and guidance. Look at what is behind His saying {which a thirsty one thinks is water}; the thirsty who suffers great thirst sees the mirage and thinks it is water, so he follows it but finds it is nothing; it rather betrayed him when he needed it most. Similarly, since the deeds of these people were not in obedience to the Messengers (PBUH) and not for the sake of Allah, they became like a mirage, they see them when they are in great thirst for them, but they find nothing therein, and they find Allah (the Exalted) who punishes them for their deeds and pays them their full due. An authentic Hadith is narrated from Abu Saied Al-Khudry[6] (may Allah be pleased with him) that the Prophet (PBUH) said in the Hadith[7] of [Allah's] manifestation on the Day of Judgment, "... Then Hell will be presented to them as if it were a mirage. Then it will be said to the Jews, 'What did you use to worship?' They will reply, 'We used to worship Ezra, the son of Allah.' It will be said to them, 'You are liars, for Allah has neither a wife nor a son. What do you want (now)?' They will reply, 'We want You to provide us with water.' Then it will be said to them 'Drink,' and they will fall down in Hell (instead). Then it will be said to the Christians, 'What did you use to worship?' They will reply, 'We used to worship Messiah (Christ), the son of Allah.' It will be said, 'You are liars, for Allah has neither a wife nor a son. What: do you want (now)?' They will say, 'We want You to provide us with water.' It will be said to them, 'Drink,' and they will fall down in Hell (instead) ... until the end of the Hadith." Such is the state of the followers of every false belief; it betrays him in the time of his most dire need. Falsehood has no reality; it is, as the name suggests, false. If the belief is neither consistent nor true, everything reliant on it is nullified. In

---

[6] One of Mohammad PBUH Companions
[7] Sahih Al Bukhari

addition, if the purpose of the deed is false, such as deeds performed for someone other than Allah or not in accordance to His commands, the deed is nullified through the nullification of its purpose, and its performer is harmed by its nullification and the occurrence of the opposite of his aim. His deeds and belief became neither for him nor against him, and he became rather tormented by the loss of their benefit and the occurrence of its opposite. That is why He (the Almighty) said {but finds Allah before Him, and He will pay him in full his due; and Allah is swift in account.} This metaphor is for the misguided who thinks he stands on guidance.

The second type are those in the stacked darkness's analogy. These people are those who knew the truth and guidance but preferred the darkness of falsehood and perversion to them and accumulated on them are the darkness of the innate disposition, the darkness of the self, the darkness of ignorance accumulated thereon, as they did not benefit from their knowledge becoming ignorant, and the darkness of following temptation and inclination. They are like one who is in an unfathomable sea with no shore, and he is covered by waves that are covered by waves that are covered by dark clouds. Thus, he is under the darkness of the sea, the darkness of the waves and the darkness of the clouds. This is analogous to the darkness's they are in from which Allah did not bring them out in to the light of faith. These two analogies, of the mirage that is imagined to be the essence of life and of the darkness that is opposite to the light, are parallel to the two analogies Allah gave to the hypocrites and the believers, meaning the analogy of water and the analogy of fire, where Allah made the believers' share thereof life and illumination, and the hypocrites' share thereof darkness–the opposite of life, and death–the opposite of life. Similarly, for the disbelievers in these two analogies, their share of water is the mirage, which deludes the observer while having no reality, and their share in the other analogy is accumulated darkness. The intent behind this may be to indicate the state of every group of disbelievers and that they are deprived of the essence of life and light by straying from the revelation, meaning that the two analogies describe the same entity. Alternatively, it may aim to indicate the diversity of the states of disbelievers, where the first analogy describes those who worked without knowledge or insight, but rather with ignorance and blind imitation of ancestor, thinking they are doing well in work, while the second analogy describes those who preferred perversion to guidance and falsehood to truth, closed their eyes to them after witnessing them, and denying them after recognizing them. The latter is those who evoked the anger of Allah and the former is those who went astray. Both groups are in contrast to those upon whom Allah have bestowed favor, who are mentioned in Allah's saying:

{اللّهُ نُورُ السَّمَاوَاتِ وَالأَرْضِ مَثَلُ نُورِهِ كَمِشْكَاةٍ فِيهَا مِصْبَاحٌ الْمِصْبَاحُ فِي زُجَاجَةٍ ...} إلى قوله (لِيَجْزِيَهُمُ اللّهُ أَحْسَنَ مَا عَمِلُوا [وَيَزِيدَهُمْ مِنْ فَضْلِهِ وَاللّهُ يَرْزُقُ مَنْ يَشَاءُ بِغَيْرِ حِسَابٍ} [النور:35-38

{Allah is the Light of the heavens and the earth. The example of His light is like a niche within which is a lamp, the lamp is within glass ...} until His saying, {That Allah may reward them [according to] the best of what they did and increase them from His bounty. And Allah gives provision to whom He wills without account.} [24:35-38]

The verses included descriptions of the three groups, namely the people of the light, the misguided–the people of the mirage, and those who invoked the anger of Allah–the people of the accumulated darkness. Allah knows best. Therefore, the first of the two analogies are for those of nullified deeds that reap no benefit, and the second is for those of useless knowledge, theories, and research that reap no benefit. The former is those of worthless deeds, and the latter are those of futile deeds. Both are opposite to the guidance and the religion of truth. That is why he compared the second group, in the clashing of the waves of doubt, suspicion and corrupt knowledge in their hearts, to the clashing of the sea waves therein and that they are stacked waves covered by dark clouds. Such are the waves of doubt and suspicion in their dark hearts, above which accumulated the clouds of allurement, inclination, and falsehood. The wise should ponder upon the states of each group and compare them to the two analogies to realize the magnificence and exaltedness of the Holy Qur'an and that it is a revelation from a Lord who is Wise and Praiseworthy. He (the Exalted) stated that what necessitated this is that He did not grant them a light, but He rather left them in the darkness in which they were created and did not bring them out to the light, since He (the Exalted) is ally of the believers; He brings them out from darkness's into the light. It Hadith is narrated in the Musnad[8] from Abdullah ibn

Umar (may Allah be pleased with them), that the Prophet (PBUH) said, "Indeed Allah (the Exalted, the Majestic) created His creation in darkness, then He cast His Light upon them, so whoever is touched by that light he is guided, and whoever is not, he goes astray. It is for this reason that I say that the pens have dried with Allah's knowledge." Allah (the Exalted) created His creation in darkness. Whoever wants His guidance, Allah will make for him an existential light, which revives his heart and soul as his body is revived with the soul that He breathed into him. These are two lives: a life for the body with the soul, and a life for the soul and heart with the light. This is why Allah called the revelation 'an inspiration', due to the reliance of the real life upon it, as He (the Almighty) said:

{يُنَزِّلُ الْمَلَائِكَةَ بِالرُّوحِ مِنْ أَمْرِهِ عَلَى مَنْ يَشَاءُ مِنْ عِبَادِهِ ...}
[النحل:2]

{He sends down the angels, with the inspiration of His command, upon whom He wills of His servants ...} [16:2]

And said:

{... يُلْقِي الرُّوحَ مِنْ أَمْرِهِ عَلَى مَنْ يَشَاءُ مِنْ عِبَادِهِ ...} [غافر:15]

{... He places the inspiration of His command upon whom He wills of His servants ...} [40:15]

And said:

{وَكَذَلِكَ أَوْحَيْنَا إِلَيْكَ رُوحًا مِنْ أَمْرِنَا مَا كُنْتَ تَدْرِي مَا الْكِتَابُ وَلَا الْإِيمَانُ وَلَكِنْ جَعَلْنَاهُ نُورًا نَهْدِي بِهِ مَنْ نَشَاءُ مِنْ عِبَادِنَا} [الشورى:52]

---

[8] Musnad is Hadith collection book by Imam Ahmad Ibn Hanbil, the same Hadith is mentioned in sunnan at-Tirmidhi

{And thus, we have revealed to you an inspiration of Our command. You did not know what the Book is or [what is] faith, but We have made it a light by which We guide whom We will of Our servants ...} [42:52]

Thus, He made His revelation an inspiration and a light; whoever is not revived by this soul is dead, and whoever is not granted of this light is in the darkness without any light

Al-Furqan 25:40

Another analogy is Allah's saying:

{أَمْ تَحْسَبُ أَنَّ أَكْثَرَهُمْ يَسْمَعُونَ أَوْ يَعْقِلُونَ إِنْ هُمْ إِلَّا كَالْأَنْعَامِ بَلْ هُمْ أَضَلُّ سَبِيلاً}
[الفرقان:44]

{Or do you think that most of them hear or reason? They are not except like livestock. Rather, they are [even] more astray in [their] way.} [25:44]

He compared most people to livestock, and the similarity between the two sides is their equivalence in not accepting guidance and following it. He made most of them more astray than livestock because the animal is guided by its herder, so it accepts the guidance and follows the road, not straying to the left or to the right. However, the majority of people are invited by the Messengers and guided to the way, but they do not comply, accept the guidance or distinguish the harmful from the beneficial, while the livestock know the difference between the harmful and the beneficial of plants and routes, avoid the former and choose the latter. Allah (the Almighty) did not grant hearts to these animals for reasoning or tongues for speech, while he gave that to these people, but they did not benefit from the minds, hearts, tongues, hearings and sights granted to them. Therefore, they are more astray than livestock, for he who is not guided to the right course and proper way while having a guide is worse and more astray than he who is not guided without having a guide.

Ar-Rum 30:28

Another metaphor is the saying of Allah (the Almighty):

{ضَرَبَ لَكُمْ مَثَلاً مِنْ أَنْفُسِكُمْ هَلْ لَكُمْ مِنْ مَا مَلَكَتْ أَيْمَانُكُمْ مِنْ شُرَكَاءَ فِي مَا رَزَقْنَاكُمْ فَأَنْتُمْ فِيهِ سَوَاءٌ تَخَافُونَهُمْ كَخِيفَتِكُمْ أَنْفُسَكُمْ كَذَلِكَ نُفَصِّلُ الآيَاتِ لِقَوْمٍ يَعْقِلُونَ} [الروم:28]

{He presents to you an example from yourselves. Do you have among those whom your right hands possess any partners in what We have provided for you so that you are equal therein [and] would fear them as your fear of one another [within a partnership]? Thus do We detail the verses for a people who use reason.} [30:28]

This is a standard argument that Allah used against the polytheists, since they made from among His servants and subjects associates to Him, so he established against them an argument, which they know to be sound and for the understanding of which they need no one else. A very eloquent argument is to take from within the person and argue against him with something known and certain to him. Thus, He told them, "Do you have among those whom your right hands possess, such as slaves and bondmaids, partners in your wealth and family?" That is to say, "Does your slaves have a share in your wealth and family, wherein you are equals, and you fear that they share equally in your wealth and take some of it as their own, as one fears his/her partner?" Ibn Abbas[9] said, "[It means] fearing that they may inherit your wealth as you inherit the wealth of one another." The meaning behind this is: Does any of you accept his slave to be a partner in his fortune and family, equal to him in authority of disposal thereof, fearing that he might dispose of some of that wealth on his own, as one fears from partners who are free? If you do not accept that for yourselves, why did you put as equals to Me some of My creation who are owned by Me? If such equation is rejected by your nature and your minds, despite being possible for you and accepted in regard to you because these slaves are not truly your own, for they are your brethren whom Allah placed under your authority and both of you are servants to Allah, so how can you accept such equation in regard to Me, despite the fact that those whom you associated with Me are My servants, My property and My creation? This is how the signs are detailed for those with intellect.

---

[9] He was the son of Al-'Abbas ibn 'Abd al-Muttalib, an uncle of prophet PBUH

CHAPTER 9

An-Nhal 16:75-76

Another analogy is the saying of Allah (the Almighty):

{ضَرَبَ اللَّهُ مَثَلاً عَبْدًا مَمْلُوكًا لاَ يَقْدِرُ عَلَى شَيْءٍ وَمَنْ رَزَقْنَاهُ مِنَّا رِزْقًا حَسَنًا فَهُوَ يُنْفِقُ مِنْهُ سِرًّا وَجَهْرًا هَلْ يَسْتَوُونَ الْحَمْدُ لِلَّهِ بَلْ أَكْثَرُهُمْ لاَ يَعْلَمُونَ} {وَضَرَبَ اللَّهُ مَثَلاً رَجُلَيْنِ أَحَدُهُمَا أَبْكَمُ لاَ يَقْدِرُ عَلَى شَيْءٍ وَهُوَ كَلٌّ عَلَى مَوْلاَهُ أَيْنَمَا يُوَجِّهْهُ لاَ يَأْتِ بِخَيْرٍ هَلْ يَسْتَوِي هُوَ وَمَنْ يَأْمُرُ بِالْعَدْلِ وَهُوَ عَلَى صِرَاطٍ مُسْتَقِيمٍ} [النحل:75-76]

{Allah presents an example: a slave [who is] owned and unable to do a thing and he to whom We have provided from Us good provision, so he spends from it secretly and publicly. Can they be equal? Praise to Allah ! But most of them do not know.} {And Allah presents an example of two men, one of them dumb and unable to do a thing, while he is a burden to his guardian. Wherever he directs him, he brings no good. Is he equal to one who commands justice, while he is on a straight path?} [16:75-76]

These two metaphors include two inverse analogies, which disprove the conclusion by disproving its introduction. There are two types of analogies: a direct analogy, which proves the conclusion by validating the correlation between the introductions, and an inverse analogy, which disproves the conclusion by invalidating the correlation between the introductions. The first metaphor is given by Allah regarding Himself and the idols. He (the Exalted) is the owner of everything; He spends as He wills on His servants, in secret and in openness, day and night. His right hand is full, no expenditure diminishes what is therein; glory is due to Him day and night. On the other hand, the idols are owned, helpless and capable of nothing, so how can you make them associates with Me and worship them beside Me, despite this great disparity and clear difference? This is the view of Mujahid and others, Ibn Abbas said, "This is an analogy given by Allah for the believer and the disbeliever. The believer is like the generous, who is provided good provision from Allah's bounty, so he spends from it, on himself and on others, secretly and publicly, and the disbeliever is like a slave who is helpless and unable to do anything, because he has nothing. Can the two men be regarded equal by any wise man? The first view is more authentic, because it is clearer in the falsity of polytheism, more obvious for the addressed, stronger in establishing the argument and in a closer accordance to Allah's saying:

{وَيَعْبُدُونَ مِنْ دُونِ اللّٰهِ مَا لاَ يَمْلِكُ لَهُمْ رِزْقًا مِنَ السَّمَاوَاتِ وَالأَرْضِ شَيْئًا وَلاَ يَسْتَطِيعُونَ} {فَلاَ تَضْرِبُوا لِلّٰهِ الأَمْثَالَ إِنَّ اللّٰهَ يَعْلَمُ وَأَنْتُمْ لاَ تَعْلَمُونَ} [النحل:73-74]

{And they worship besides Allah that which does not possess for them [the power of] provision from the heavens and the earth at all, and [in fact], they are unable.} {So, do not assert similarities to Allah. Indeed, Allah knows, and you do not know.} [16:73-74]

After which Allah said {Allah presents an example: a slave [who is] owned and unable ...}. This analogy necessitates that the monotheist believer is like the one who is provided good provision and the polytheist disbeliever is like the slave who is owned and unable to do anything. This is indicated by the analogy, so Ibn Abbas stated it pointing to it as the verse's denotation, because it is distinctive to the verse. Take note of this because you will find it frequently in the speech of Ibn Abbas and other early scholars in interpreting the Holy Qur'an, and one might think that this is the sole meaning of the verse and narrate it from him as such.

As for the second metaphor, it is an analogy given by Allah (the Exalted) for Himself and for those they worship beside Him. The idol worshipped beside Allah is like a dumb person who neither understands nor speaks and is of a mute heart and tongue. He is deprived of the speech of the heart and the tongue, and above that, he is helpless and can do nothing whatsoever. In addition, wherever you direct him, he brings no good nor fulfils a need. Allah (the Almighty), on the other hand, is Alive, Capable, Speaking, who commands Justice, and is on a Straight Way. This describes Him with the utmost perfection and praise, because His commanding of justice, when it is the right way, entails that He (the Exalted) knows it, informs of it, endorses it, commands His servants to do it, loves its people and does not command otherwise; He is even considered too exalted for its opposites, which are injustice, unfairness, weak-mindedness and falsehood. All His commands and provisions are entirely just, and the people of justice are His allies, loved ones and those seated on His right side on "Minbars" Pulpit of light. His commanding of justice involves the religious legal command and the universal fatalistic command; both of them are entirely just, as the authentic Hadith states: "O Allah, I am Your slave, the son of Your slave and the son of Your female slave, my forelock is in Your grasp, Your decree in me is enforced, Your fate in me is just ..." Thus, His fate is his universal command, His command is only when He intends a thing that He says to it, "Be," and it is. He does not command except what is just and true; the fate and destiny of which He is the Maintainer is just and true. If the fateful and the predestined contained that which is not fair or just, then the fate is different from the fateful and the destiny is different from the predestined. Then He (the Exalted) informed that {He is on a straight path}, which is parallel to the saying of Shu'ayb[10] (PBUH):

{إِنِّي تَوَكَّلْتُ عَلَى اللّٰهِ رَبِّي وَرَبِّكُمْ مَّا مِنْ دَابَّةٍ إِلَّا هُوَ آخِذٌ بِنَاصِيَتِهَا إِنَّ رَبِّي عَلَى صِرَاطٍ مُسْتَقِيمٍ} [هود:56]

{Indeed, I have relied upon Allah, my Lord and your Lord. There is no creature but that He holds its forelock. Indeed, my Lord is on a path [that is] straight.} [11:56]

---

[10] [Note from the Translator: This is actually a mistake, because this is the saying of Hud (PBUH) and not Shu'ayb (PBUH).]

Therefore, saying {There is no creature but that He holds its forelock} is parallel to saying, "my forelock is in Your grasp", and saying {Indeed, my Lord is on a path [that is] straight} is parallel to saying, "Your fate in me is just". The former is His dominion, and the latter is His praise, for to Him (the Exalted) belongs dominion, and to Him belongs [all] praise. Being on the straight path entails that He does not speak except the truth, does not command except what is just and does not do except what is good, wise and fair. Thus, He is right in His words and deeds; He does not judge him unfairly, does not hold him accountable for the mistakes of others, does not reduce any of his good deeds, does not burden him with sins he did not commit or contribute towards, does not impose blame on someone for the sins of another, and does not do anything that is not praiseworthy and of good consequence and desirable ends. His being on the straight path disallows any of that.

Muhammad ibn Jarir Al-Tabary[11] said, "His saying: {Indeed, my Lord is on a path [that is] straight} means: My Lord is on the path of truth; He rewards the good among His creation for his good deeds and the evil for his evil deeds; He does injustice to no one and does not accept from them except Islam and belief." Then he narrated from Shibl, from Ibn Abu Nageih, that Mujahid said in interpreting the phrase {Indeed, my Lord is on a

---

[11] One of the Great Muslims scholars with many great books

path [that is] straight}, "The right path," and so was narrated from him by Ibn Juraij. Some said that this is like His saying:

{إِنَّ رَبَّكَ لَبِالْمِرْصَادِ} [الفجر:14]

{Indeed, your Lord is in observation.} [89:14]

This is merely a difference in expression, because being in observation entails rewarding the good for his good deeds and the evil for his evil deeds. Another group said that the phrase contains an omission which is estimated to be {Indeed, my Lord encourages and motivate you to be on a path [that is] straight}. If they wanted to say that this is the meaning behind the verse, then their claim is wrong and there is no evidence for such an omission.

He (the Exalted) differentiated between His being a commander of justice and being on the straight path. If they wanted to say that His encouraging being on the straight path is entailed in His being on the straight path, then they are correct. A third group said that His being on the straight path means that all creatures and matters return to Allah without missing anything thereof. If these people wished to say that this is the meaning of the verse then they are wrong, but if they wanted to say that this is a requirement of His being on the straight path then they are correct. Another group said that it means that everything is under His power, control, dominion and grasp. This, however true, is not the meaning of the verse. Shu'ayb (PBUH) differentiated between his saying {There is no creature but that He holds its forelock} and his saying {Indeed, my Lord is on a path [that is] straight}. They are two independent ideas.

Therefore, the correct view is Mujahid's view, which is the view of the leaders of Qur'anic interpretation, and the Arabic language does not have capacity for another interpretation except forcefully. Jarir[12] said, in praise of Umar ibn Abd Al-Aziz[13]:

Amir Al-Mu'minin is on a path   Which, even if the roads twisted, is straight

He (the Almighty) also said:

{ ... مَنْ يَشَإِ اللَّهُ يُضْلِلْهُ وَمَنْ يَشَأْ يَجْعَلْهُ عَلَى صِرَاطٍ مُسْتَقِيمٍ}
[الأنعام:39]

{... Whomever Allah wills - He leaves astray; and whomever He wills - He puts him on a straight path.} [6:39]

If he (the Almighty) is the one who made His Messengers (PBUT) and their followers on the straight path in their words and deeds, then He (the Exalted) is more worthy of being on the straight path in His words and deeds. If the straight path of the Messengers and their followers is to comply with His command, His straight path is what is necessitated by His praise, perfection and glory of speaking the truth and exercising it. Success if from Allah.

There is another view in the verse, just like the first verse, that this analogy is given for the believer and the disbeliever.

---

[12] Famous Arab poet lived in Umayyad time
[13] an Umayyad caliph who ruled from 717 to 720, even his reign was very short (three years), he is very highly regarded in Muslim World, and Many scholar count his as the Fifth of the Rashidun Caliphate.

We have already discussed this interpretation. Success if from Allah.

Al-Muddathir 74:49-51

Another analogy is the Saying of Allah (the Almighty) regarding those who turned away from His words and pondering over them:

{فَمَا لَهُمْ عَنِ التَّذْكِرَةِ مُعْرِضِينَ} {كَأَنَّهُمْ حُمُرٌ مُسْتَنْفِرَةٌ} {فَرَّتْ مِنْ قَسْوَرَةٍ} [المدثر:49-51]

{Then what is [the matter] with them that they are, from the reminder, turning away} {As if they were alarmed zebras} {Fleeing from a lion?} [74:49-51]

He compared them in their turning away and repulsion from the Holy Qur'an like zebras that saw a lion or a hunter and escaped from them. This is a wonderful comparison, as those people, in their ignorance of what Allah sent His Messengers to convey, are like zebras, which cannot understand. However, if they hear the voice of the lion or a hunter they are scared away strongly. This is a very intense dispraise for these people, because they escape from the guidance that contains their happiness and life as zebras run escape from what kills and butchers them. The word 'مستنفرة (alarmed)' here is more eloquent than 'نافرة (fleeing)', because due to the intensity of their fear, they alarm one another and encourage one another to flee[14].

---

[14] [Note from translator: This part until the remainder of the paragraph discusses Arabic Verbatim and the subtle difference in meaning that the changes in word structure cause. It is very difficult and somewhat pointless to translate it to a non-native speaker of Arabic.]

CHAPTER 11

Al-Jumu'a 62:5

Another analogy is the saying of Allah (the Almighty):

{مَثَلُ الَّذِينَ حُمِّلُوا التَّوْرَاةَ ثُمَّ لَمْ يَحْمِلُوهَا كَمَثَلِ الْحِمَارِ يَحْمِلُ أَسْفَارًا بِئْسَ مَثَلُ الْقَوْمِ الَّذِينَ كَذَّبُوا بِآيَاتِ اللَّهِ وَاللَّهُ لاَ يَهْدِي الْقَوْمَ الظَّالِمِينَ} [الجمعة:5]

{The example of those who were entrusted with the Torah and then did not take it on is like that of a donkey who carries volumes [of books]. Wretched is the example of the people who deny the signs of Allah . And Allah does not guide the wrongdoing people.} [62:5]

He (the Exalted) likened those He entrusted to bear His book to believe in it, ponder upon it, apply it and invite to it but contradicted all that and only bore it by memorization without pondering upon it, understanding it, following it, seeking its judgment or behaving in accordance to it, to the donkey carrying volumes of books without knowing what is inside it; its only share thereof is carrying it on its back. Thus, their only share of

the book of Allah is like this donkey's share of the books on its
back. This metaphor, despite being given for the Jews, applies in
its essence to those who bore the Qur'an but ignored applying it,
did not fulfil its responsibilities and did not observe it with due
observance.

CHAPTER 12

Al-A'raf 7:175-176

Another metaphor is the saying of Allah (the Almighty):

﴿وَاتْلُ عَلَيْهِمْ نَبَأَ الَّذِي آتَيْنَاهُ آيَاتِنَا فَانْسَلَخَ مِنْهَا فَأَتْبَعَهُ الشَّيْطَانُ فَكَانَ مِنَ الْغَاوِينَ﴾ ﴿وَلَوْ شِئْنَا لَرَفَعْنَاهُ بِهَا وَلَكِنَّهُ أَخْلَدَ إِلَى الْأَرْضِ وَاتَّبَعَ هَوَاهُ فَمَثَلُهُ كَمَثَلِ الْكَلْبِ إِنْ تَحْمِلْ عَلَيْهِ يَلْهَثْ أَوْ تَتْرُكْهُ يَلْهَثْ ذَلِكَ مَثَلُ الْقَوْمِ الَّذِينَ كَذَّبُوا بِآيَاتِنَا فَاقْصُصِ الْقَصَصَ لَعَلَّهُمْ يَتَفَكَّرُونَ﴾ [الأعراف:175-176]

{And recite to them, [O Muhammad], the news of him to whom we gave [knowledge of] Our signs, but he detached himself from them; so Satan pursued him, and he became of the deviators.} {And if We had willed, We could have elevated him thereby, but he adhered [instead] to the earth and followed his own desire. So his example is like that of the dog: if you chase him, he pants, or if you leave him, he [still] pants. That is the example of the people who denied Our signs. So relate the stories that perhaps they will give thought.} [7:175-176]

He (the Exalted) compared those whom He gave His book and taught the knowledge He deprived others but they ignored applying them, followed their own inclinations and preferred Allah's wrath to His satisfaction, the worldly life to the Hereafter and the created to the Creator, He compared those to the dog, which is one of the most dark, lowly and malicious animals, the enthusiasm of which does not go beyond its stomach; a very gluttonous and greedy animal, so much so that it does not walk except with his nose to the ground snuffling and sniffing in gluttony and greed. It smells its bum more often than any other of its body parts. If you throw a stone to it, it goes to it and bites it gluttonously. It is one of the most menial and humble animals and of the most accepting of inferiorities. A smelly cadaver is dearer to it than soft meat, and dirt is dearer to it than fruits are. If it got a cadaver sufficient for a hundred dogs, it would not allow a single dog to eat anything with it without rebuking and scolding it out of greed and avarice. One of its strange traits of its gluttony is that if it saw someone with a shabby outlook, raged clothes and a poor state, it barks and charges at him, as if it imagines being commensurate and equal to him in stature, and if it saw someone with a good outlook, beautiful clothes and authority, it places its head on the ground, submits to him and does not raise its head. Comparing whoever prefers the worldly life and its quick pleasures to Allah and the Hereafter, despite being versed in knowledge to the dog in its panting contains a wonderful subtle point: The person mentioned by Allah who detached himself from Allah's verses and who follows his whims is very strong in yearning for the worldly life due to the severance of his heart from Allah and the Hereafter. He yearns strongly for it, and his yearning resembles the dog's panting whether being pestered or left alone. Yearning and panting are close to one another in pronunciation and in meaning[15]. Ibn Juraij said, "The dog is devoid of heart; it pants if you chase it and it pants if you leave it. In that regard, it is like the one who turns away from the guidance; he is devoid of heart." By that, he means that the dog has no heart to drive it to patience and prevent it from panting; similarly, the one who detached himself from the verses of Allah has no heart to encourage him to persevere in this worldly life and avoid over-eagerness for it. The latter yearns for the worldly life due to his lack of patience, and the former pants due to his lack of tolerance for lack of water. The dog is among the least thirst-enduring animals; if it thirsts, it licks the dust, even if it can endure hunger. In any case, it is among the most panting animals; it pants standing, sitting, walking and stopping. This is due to its intense greed; the heat of greed in its liver forces him to pant continuously. Similarly, for the person compared to it, the heat of desire in his heart forces him to pant relentlessly; if you pester him with admonishment and advice, he pants, and if you leave him without admonishment, he yearns. Mujahid said, "This is the metaphor of the one who was given the book and did not apply it." Ibn Abbas said, "[It means] If you burden him with the word, he does not bear it, and if you leave him, he is not guided to the right way; like the dog, it pants when it is lying

---

[15] Referring to the Arabic terms of course.

down, and it pants when it is being chased." Al-Hassan said, "[It refers to] the hypocrite, who does not stand firm upon the truth, whether he is invited or not, like the dog that pants whether chased away or left alone."

Ataa'[16] said, "It barks whether you chase it away or not." Muhammad ibn Qutaibah[17] said, "Everything that pants do so out of exhaustion or thirst, except the dog; it pants whether tired or rested, whether healthy or ill, whether thirsty or not. Thus, Allah compared it to those who disbelieve in His signs." Ibn Atiyyah said, "He is astray whether you admonish him or not. Therefore, he is like the dog, which pants whether you chase it away or leave it alone. This is parallel to Allah's (the Almighty) saying:

$$\{وَإِنْ تَدْعُوهُمْ إِلَى الْهُدَى لاَ يَتَّبِعُوكُمْ سَوَاءٌ عَلَيْكُمْ أَدَعَوْتُمُوهُمْ أَمْ أَنْتُمْ صَامِتُونَ\} [الأعراف:193]$$

{And if you [believers] invite them to guidance, they will not follow you. It is all the same for you whether you invite them or you are silent.} [7:193]"

Observe what this analogy contains of wisdom and denotation. For example, Allah's saying {to whom we gave [knowledge of] Our signs}, so He (the Exalted) informed that He was the one who gave him the knowledge, so it is a bounty from Allah, and Allah is the one who blessed him with it, so he

---

[16] One of Muslims scholars specialized in Hadith
[17] One of Muslims scholars specialized in Hadith

attributed it to Himself. Then He said {but he detached himself from them}, meaning he got out of them like the snake sheds its skin and parted with them like skin separated from the flesh. He did not say {We detached him from them} because he was the one who cause such detachment by following his inclination. Another example is Allah's saying {so Satan pursued him}, meaning he caught up with him and reached him, as Allah (the Almighty) said about the people of Pharoah:

{فَأَتْبَعُوهُمْ مُشْرِقِينَ} [الشعراء:60]

{So they pursued them at sunrise.} [26:60]

Thus, he was protected and guarded by the verses of Allah from Satan, out of his reach except unaware and in a flash. However, when he detached himself from the verses of Allah, Satan caught him as a lion catches its prey, so he became of the deviators who do not practice their knowledge and who know the truth but behave contradictorily, like the scholars of evil. Another example is Allah's (the Exalted) saying {And if We had willed, We could have elevated him thereby}, so He (the Exalted) stated that elevation by Him is not merely because of knowledge, for this person was a scholar, but rater through following the truth, giving preference to it and seeking the satisfaction of Allah (the Almighty). This man was among the most knowledgeable of his time, and Allah did not elevate him and did not benefit him with it. Thus, ask Allah for refuge from knowledge that is of no benefit. He (the Exalted) stated that He is the one who elevates His servant if He willed with what He granted him of knowledge. If Allah did not elevate him, then he is degraded, brining pride to no one, because Allah, the Abaser and the Exalter, abased him and did not exalt him. It means: Had WE willed, we could have preferred him, honored him and raised his rank and stature with the verses We had granted him. Ibn Abbas (may Allah be pleased with them) said, "Had We willed, we would have raised him with his knowledge thereof." Another group said that the hidden pronoun in {We could have elevated him thereby} refers to disbelief, meaning: Had We willed, we could have elevated and protected him from disbelief by what he had of Our verses. Mujahid and Ataa' said, "[It means] we could have elevated the disbelief from him with belief and protected him." This interpretation is correct. The first interpretation is the intent of the verse, and this one is a requirement for such intent. We have already stated that the Early Muslims often pointed out to a requirement of the verse's intent and some might think that this is the intent. Regarding His saying {but he adhered [instead] to the earth}, Ibn Jubair[18] said, "[It means] he inclined towards the earth," Mujahid[19] said, "He resided therein," and Muqatil[20] said, "He became content with the worldly life." Abu Ubaidah[21] said, "He clung to it and slowed down [22]...

---

[18] One of early Muslims scholars specialized in explaining the Holy Quran
[19] One of the famous scholar in Quran studies he was taught by Mohammad PBUH Companions
[20] One the Tafseer scholar
[21] One of Mohammad PBUH Companion and one the ten Companions Promised Paradise in their life
[22] [Note from translator: The rest of this paragraph and the following one until 'فلا ينافي القولين' discuss Arabic Verbatim and linguistics as well as the origins of the word 'أخلد', translated here as 'adhered'. It is very difficult and somewhat pointless to translate it to a non-native speaker of Arabic.]

Regarding His saying {and followed his own desire}, Al-Kalby[23] said, "[It means] he followed the trivial matters and ignored the great ones." Abu Rawq[24] said, "He preferred the worldly life to the Hereafter." Ataa' said, "He desired the worldly life and obeyed his devil." Ibn Zaid said, "His desire was with those people," meaning the ones who fought against Moses (PBUH) and his people. Yaman said, "He followed his wife because she was the one who incited him to do what he did." If someone said, "Using the contrasting conjunction 'but' necessitates to confirm after it what was denied before it or vice versa, such as saying 'If I had wished, I would have given him, but I did not,' or 'If I wished, I would not have done so-and-so, but I did'. Therefore, the contrasting conjunction necessitates saying {And if We had willed, We could have elevated him thereby, but We did not will so} or {but We did not elevate him, but he adhered. So how did He use {but he adhered [instead] to the earth} after saying {And if We had willed, We could have elevated him thereby}?" The answer is, "This is a case of the speech when the meaning is obvious, and the words are forewent. Such is the essence of His saying {And if We had willed, We could have elevated him thereby}, that he did not follow the causes that lead to elevating him by the verses, such as preferring Allah and pleasing Him to his desires, but he preferred the worldly life, adhered to the earth and followed his desire." Al-Zamakhshary[25] said, "It means if he adhered to our

_____

[23] One of the Imams in Tafseer
[24] Scholar in Tafseer
[25] A great scholar in Islam and Arabic Language

verses, we would have raised him thereby. He stated the will [of Allah], but the intent is what that will stems and results from." Do you not observe His saying {But he adhered}? He negated the will by his [the man's] adherence, which is his [the man's] action. Thus, {if We had willed} must mean what he [the man] did. Otherwise, it should have been said {if We had willed, we could have raised him, but we did not." This is a known habit of a Qadari who denies the general will of Allah and who is mistaken in making the word of Allah's Mu'tazili[26] and Qadari[27].

How does His saying {And if We had willed} relate to the saying {if he adhered to our verses}? If such adherence was reliant on the will of Allah, which is the truth, then his interpretation is invalid. His saying that the will of Allah results from the man's adherence to the verses, which [in turn] is dependent on the will of Allah, then the will of Allah is the leader, not the follower, the cause, not the effect, and a prerequisite, not a subsequent. What Allah wills must exist, and what He does not will must not exist.

---

[26] Mu'tazili: a school of theology, which give precedence to the logical evidence over the revelation, and refuse the Hadiths that contradict logic, from their perspective.

[27] Qadari: a deviant sect of Islam, which state that Allah has no knowledge of incidents until they occur, and that the happenings are due to the will of humans, not the will of Allah

Al-Hujurat 49:12

Another metaphor is the saying of Allah (the Almighty):

{يَا أَيُّهَا الَّذِينَ آمَنُوا اجْتَنِبُوا كَثِيرًا مِنَ الظَّنِّ إِنَّ بَعْضَ الظَّنِّ إِثْمٌ وَلَا تَجَسَّسُوا وَلَا يَغْتَبْ بَعْضُكُمْ بَعْضًا أَيُحِبُّ أَحَدُكُمْ أَنْ يَأْكُلَ لَحْمَ أَخِيهِ مَيْتًا فَكَرِهْتُمُوهُ وَاتَّقُوا اللَّهَ إِنَّ اللَّهَ تَوَّابٌ رَحِيمٌ} [الحجرات:12]

{O you who have believed, avoid much [negative] assumption. Indeed, some assumption is sin. And do not spy or backbite each other. Would one of you like to eat the flesh of his brother when dead? You would detest it. And fear Allah ; indeed, Allah is Accepting of repentance and Merciful.} [49:12]

This is a highly representative analogy, because He compared tearing up the brother's reputation to ripping apart his flesh. Since the backbiter tears up the reputation of his brother in his absence, he is like someone who rips apart his flesh in the absence of his soul, meaning death. Since the victim of backbiting is unable to defend himself due to his absence, he is like the dead whose flesh is torn apart while unable to defend himself. In addition, since the essence of brotherhood is mutual mercy, maintenance and aid, and the backbiter goes against that essence through defamation, criticism and slander, this is parallel to ripping apart the flesh of his brother, when brotherhood necessitates protecting, mandating and defending him. Since the backbiter enjoys his backbiting and defamation and amuses himself with that, he is likened to one who eats the flesh of his brother after ripping it apart, and since the backbiter likes that and is fond of it, he is compared to someone who likes eating the flesh of his dead brother. Such liking exceeds the mere act of eating, just as eating exceeds the mere act of ripping it apart. Thus, observe this comparison and analogy, its good representation and the correspondence of the intelligible to the perceivable therein. Look closely at His informing about their detestation of eating the flesh of the dead brother, with which he described them at the end of the verse, and denouncing in its beginning those of them who like that. If this is disapproved in their nature, how can they like what is similar and parallel to it? He argued with what they detested against what they liked, and compared what they like with what is most disgusting and repulsive for them. Thus, intellect, pure nature and wisdom necessitate that they be as repulsed as can be from what is similar and parallel to it. Success is from Allah.

CHAPTER 14

Ibrahim 14:18

Another metaphor is the saying of Allah (the Almighty):

﴿مَثَلُ الَّذِينَ كَفَرُوا بِرَبِّهِمْ أَعْمَالُهُمْ كَرَمَادٍ اشْتَدَّتْ بِهِ الرِّيحُ فِي يَوْمٍ عَاصِفٍ لَا يَقْدِرُونَ مِمَّا كَسَبُوا عَلَى شَيْءٍ ذَلِكَ هُوَ الضَّلَالُ الْبَعِيدُ﴾ [إبراهيم:18]

{The example of those who disbelieve in their Lord is [that] their deeds are like ashes which the wind blows forcefully on a stormy day; they are unable [to keep] from what they earned a [single] thing. That is what extreme error is.} [14:18]

Allah (the Almighty) likened the disbelievers' deeds, in their futility and uselessness like ashes exposed to strong wind on a stormy day. He (the Almighty) likened their deeds in their invalidity, nullity and being like dispersed dust, due to having no base in faith and proficiency, to being for someone other than Allah and to not being in accordance to His commands, he likened them to ashes blown away by the stormy wind, so that its owner cannot utilize any of them in the time of his dire need. Thus, {they are unable [to keep] from what they earned a [single] thing}. On the Day of Judgment, they cannot find any of the deeds they earned, and they cannot find any effect thereof, such as a reward or a useful benefit. Allah does not accept a deed except one that is sincerely dedicated to Him, conforming to His law. There are four types of deeds: one is accepted and three are rejected. The accepted deed is the sincere and correct deed; sincere means to not be for the sake of anyone beside Allah, and correct means to be of what He ordained on the tongue of His Messenger (PBUH); the three rejected types are what contradicts that.

Comparing these deeds to ashes contain a wonderful subtle point, due to the resemblance between their deeds and the ashes in that the fire burns and eliminates the essence of both of them. The deeds that are for the sake of someone other than Allah are fodder to Hellfire; with them Hellfire is set ablaze for its residents; Allah creates for them from their invalid deeds fire and torment, just as He creates for the performers of the deeds that are in accordance to His commands and sincerely dedicated to Him pleasure and revival. Thus, the fire affected the deeds of those people until it made them ashes; they, and what they used to worship beside Allah, are fuel for Hellfire.

CHAPTER 15

Ibrahim 14:27

Another analogy is the saying of Allah (the Almighty):

{أَلَمْ تَرَ كَيْفَ ضَرَبَ اللهُ مَثَلاً كَلِمَةً طَيِّبَةً كَشَجَرَةٍ طَيِّبَةٍ أَصْلُهَا ثَابِتٌ وَفَرْعُهَا فِي السَّمَاءِ} {تُؤْتِي أُكُلَهَا كُلَّ حِينٍ بِإِذْنِ رَبِّهَا وَيَضْرِبُ اللهُ الأَمْثَالَ لِلنَّاسِ لَعَلَّهُمْ يَتَذَكَّرُونَ} {وَمَثَلُ كَلِمَةٍ خَبِيثَةٍ كَشَجَرَةٍ خَبِيثَةٍ اجْتُثَّتْ مِنْ فَوْقِ الأَرْضِ مَا لَهَا مِنْ قَرَارٍ} {يُثَبِّتُ اللهُ الَّذِينَ آمَنُوا بِالْقَوْلِ الثَّابِتِ فِي الْحَيَاةِ الدُّنْيَا وَفِي الآخِرَةِ وَيُضِلُّ اللهُ الظَّالِمِينَ وَيَفْعَلُ اللهُ مَا يَشَاءُ} [إبراهيم:24-27]

{Have you not considered how Allah presents an example, [making] a good word like a good tree, whose root is firmly fixed and its branches [high] in the sky?} {It produces its fruit all the time, by permission of its Lord. And Allah presents examples for the people that perhaps they will be reminded.} {And the example of a bad word is like a bad tree, uprooted from the surface of the earth, not having any stability.} {Allah keeps firm those who believe, with the firm word, in worldly life and in the Hereafter. And Allah sends

**astray the wrongdoers. And Allah does what He wills.}
[14:24-27]** [28]

Allah (the Exalted) compared the good word to the good tree, because the good word yields good deeds, and the good tree yields good fruits. This is clear in the view of the majority of interpreters, who say that the good word is testifying that there is no deity except Allah, because it leads to all good deeds, both hidden and apparent. Every good deed that pleases Allah (the Exalted, the Majestic) is a fruit of this word. In the interpretation of Ali ibn Talhah, he narrates that Ibn Abbas (may Allah be pleased with them) said, "{whose root is firmly fixed} refers to saying 'There is no deity except Allah' in the believer's heart. {and its branches [high] in the sky} mean that it raises the believer's deeds to heaven." Al-Rabei' ibn Anas "{a good word}: this is a metaphor for faith; faith is the good tree. Its firmly fixed root that does not go away is dedication. Its branch in the sky is the fear of Allah." The metaphor according to this interpretation is closer, clearer and better, for He (the Exalted) compared the tree of monotheism in the heart to a good tree whose roots are firmly fixed, whose branches are towering in the sky, and which yields its fruit all the time.

If you examine this analogy closely, you will find that it conforms to the monotheism tree, which is firmly rooted in the

---

[28] [Note from the translator: In the book, only the first two verses are actually stated here. However, since the book continues to talk about the other two verses without stating them, I chose to state them here for the benefit of the reader.]

heart, whose branches of good deeds rise to heaven. This tree keeps yielding good deeds all the time based on its firm rootedness in the heart, the hearts love for it, in it, knowledge of its truth, fulfilment of its responsibility, and observing it with due observance. The person in whose heart this word is firmly rooted with its reality, whose heart is characterized by it, and shaped, through it, by the religion of Allah, better than which there is no religion, so that he knows the truth of the state, which his mind affirms for Allah, for which his tongue testifies, and which his organs believe, and he denies such truth and its requirements for anyone beside Allah, and his heart joins his tongue in such denial and affirmation, and his organs submit to Him for whose oneness he testified, obeying and following the ways of his Lord laid down, not deviating from them or desiring other ways instead, as the heart does not desire another in place of the one it worships, then undoubtedly this word, from this heart, on this tongue, will keep yielding its fruit of good deeds that ascends to the Lord (the Almighty). This good word yields many good words accompanied with righteous deeds, so the righteous deeds raise the good words, as He (the Almighty) said:

{... إِلَيْهِ يَصْعَدُ الْكَلِمُ الطَّيِّبُ وَالْعَمَلُ الصَّالِحُ يَرْفَعُهُ ...} [فاطر:10]

{... To Him ascends good speech, and righteous work raises it ...} [35:10]

Thus, He (the Exalted) informed that the righteous deeds raise the good speech, and informed that the good deeds yield for its speaker good deeds all the time.

The intent is that if the believer testified with the word of [Allah's] oneness, understanding its meaning and truth positively and negatively, fulfilling its requirements, and testifying with his heart, tongue and organs, this word from this witness is firmly rooted in his heart, its branches are connected to the sky, and it yields its fruits all the time. Some of the early scholars said that the tree in the verse is the palm tree, which is proved by the authentic Hadith[29] narrated by Ibn Umar[30]. Some of them said that it refers to the believer himself, as Muhammad ibn said narrated from his father, from his uncle, from his grandfather that Ibn Abbas said, "{Have you not considered how Allah presents an example, [making] a good word like a good tree ...}: the good tree refers to the believer, and by having a firmly fixed root in the ground and branches in the sky, it means that the believer speaks and behaves on earth, and his words and deeds reach the heaven, while he is still on earth." Atiyyah Al-Awfy said regarding the verse {Have you not considered how Allah presents an example, [making] a good word like a good tree ...}, "This is a metaphor for the believer, who continues to emit good words and righteous deeds that ascend to Allah." Al-Rabei' ibn Anas, "{whose root is firmly fixed and its branches [high] in the sky}: This refers to the believer, and this is an analogy for his dedication and worship to Allah alone" Tawheed"[31] , no partner has He. {whose root is firmly fixed}:

[29] Sahih Al Bukhari
[30] One of great Companion Abdula Son of Umar
[31] Tawheed in Arabic means attributing Oneness to Allah and describing Him as being One and Unique, with no partner or peer in His Essence and

The root of his deeds is firmly fixed in the ground. "{and its branches [high] in the sky}: the mention of which takes place in the heavens." There is no difference between the two views. The intent of the metaphor is the believer, and the palm tree is likened to him and he is likened to it. If the palm tree is a good tree, the believer compared to it is worthy of being so. Some of the early scholars said, "It refers to a tree in Paradise," and the palm tree is among the most venerated trees of Paradise.

This analogy contains subtle points and knowledge as much as befits the knowledge and wisdom of its Speaker (the Exalted). For example, the tree must have roots, stem, branches, leaves and fruits. So is the tree of faith and Islam, in order for the two sides of the analogy to match. Its roots are knowledge and certainty, its stem is dedication, its branches are deeds, and its fruits are what the righteous deeds entail of positive effects, praiseworthy traits, virtuous morals, upright disposition and satisfactory guidance. Therefore, the planting of the tree in the heart and its firm rootedness are deduced from these matters. If the knowledge is correct and matches the knowledge contained in the book that Allah sent down, if the belief matches what He, as well as His Messengers (PBUT), informed about Himself, if the dedication is existent in the heart and if the deeds conform to the commands, guidance and upright disposition, similar to these roots and in harmony with them, it is confirmed that the tree of faith in the heart has firmly fixed roots in the ground and

---

Attributes.

branches in the sky. If it was the opposite, it is deduced that what exists in the heart is the bad tree, which is uprooted from the surface of the earth, not having any stability. Another example is that the tree does not survive except with a substance that irrigates and develops it, if the irrigation ceases, then it is all but dried out. So is the tree of Islam in the heart, if its owner does not continuously irrigate it with beneficial behavior, righteous deeds and moving from remembrance to consideration and vice versa, it becomes on the verge of drying out. It is narrated in Musnad Ahmad from Abu Hurairah that the Messenger (PBUH) said, "Faith becomes worn out in the heart as the dress does, so revive your faith." In general, if the plant is not maintained by the farmer it almost dies. Thus, we know the dire need of people for what Allah ordained of successive rituals over the passing times and His great mercy, complete blessing and beneficence towards His servants by imposing them and making them a substance to irrigate the monotheism plant, which He planted in their hearts.

Another example is that Allah made the norm that the useful plant must be contaminated with strange bushes and plants foreign to it. If the farmer maintains, purifies and prunes it, the plant grows perfect, firm and complete, and its fruits becomes more plentiful, better and more delicious. However, if he left these contaminants, they almost overtake and dominate the plant or weaken the original plant and make the fruits ugly and imperfect based on their frequency. Whoever has no comprehension to make this analogy and understand it will miss a lot of profit unaware. The believer continuously endeavors in two aspects: watering this tree and clearing its surroundings; by irrigation, it lasts and remains, and by purification, it grows perfect and complete. Allah is the one sought for help and in Him trust is placed.

This is some of what is contained in this great and glorious analogy of subtle points and wisdom. Perhaps this is a drop in the see according to our humble intellects, blundered hearts, incompetent knowledge and deeds that necessitate repentance and asking for forgiveness. Had our hearts become pure, had our minds become clear, had our souls become chastened, had our deeds become sincere and had our resolves been devoted for receiving [knowledge] from Allah (the Almighty) and His Messenger (PBUH), we would have witnessed of the meanings, secrets and wisdom of the speech of Allah (the Exalted, the Majestic) what diminishes the insights and fades away the knowledge of truth. This is how one realizes the standing of the Companions' knowledge (may Allah be pleased with them), and that the difference between their knowledge and the knowledge of their successors is like the difference between them in merit. Allah is most knowing of where He places His bounty and whom He selects for His mercy.

Then He (the Exalted) gave a metaphor for the bad word, so He compared it to the bad tree that is uprooted from the surface of the earth, not having any stability. Thus, it has no stable roots, no high branches, no pure fruits, no shades, no harvests, no upright stem, no root fixed in the ground. Therefore, neither is its lower part abundant, nor is its upper part graceful. It has no reap, and it is not superior, but is rather surpassed [by the other trees].

If the wise observed most of the people's words in their speech and writing, he will find it as such. The ultimate loss is standing with it and occupying oneself with it from the best and most beneficial speech. Al-Dahhak said, "Allah gave a metaphor for the disbeliever with a tree uprooted from the surface of the earth and having no stability. It has no root, branch, fruit or benefit therein. Similarly, the disbeliever does not do or say any good, and Allah does not make in him any blessing or benefit." Ibn Abbas said, "{And the example of a bad word}, which is polytheism, {is like a bad tree}, meaning the disbeliever, {uprooted from the surface of the earth, not having any stability}." He also says, "Polytheism has no root or evidence for the disbeliever to rely upon; Allah does not accept the polytheist's deeds, nor do they ascend to Allah. Thus, he has no fixed roots in the ground nor branches in the sky." He also says, "He has no righteous deeds in Heavens nor in the Hereafter." Al-Rabei' ibn Anas said, "The bad tree resembles the disbeliever; his words and deeds have no roots or branches; his words and deeds are neither firmly fixed in the ground nor elevated to Heavens." Saied narrated from Qatadah regarding this verse that a man met with a scholar and asked him, "What do you say about the bad word?" He said, "It does not have stability on the earth or elevation to the sky, except if it clung to the neck of its speaker until he is accounted for it on the Day of Judgment." His saying {uprooted} means amputate from the face of the earth. Then, He (the Exalted) informed of His bounty and justice between the two parties: people of the good word and people of the bad word. He informed that he supports the believers with the firm word when they need it most in the worldly life and the Hereafter, and that he misleads the wrongdoers, meaning the polytheists, from the firm word. Thus, He misled those with His justice, and He made firm the believers with His bounty. His saying {Allah keeps firm those who believe, with the firm word, in worldly life and in the Hereafter ...} contains a great treasure. Whoever stops at its source, perfects its extraction and acquisition, and spends from it will be successful, and whoever is deprived of it is the loser. This is because one does not do without the support of Allah for a blink of an eye. If He does not make him firm, the heavens and earth of his faith will cease to exist in their place. Allah (the Almighty) said to the most honorable of His creation, His servant and Messenger:

{وَلَوْلَا أَنْ ثَبَّتْنَاكَ لَقَدْ كِدْتَ تَرْكَنُ إِلَيْهِمْ شَيْئًا قَلِيلًا} [الإسراء:74]

{And if We had not strengthened you, you would have almost inclined to them a little.} [17:74]

He (the Almighty) also said:

{إِذْ يُوحِي رَبُّكَ إِلَى الْمَلَائِكَةِ أَنِّي مَعَكُمْ فَثَبِّتُوا الَّذِينَ آمَنُوا ...} [الأنفال:12]

{[Remember] when your Lord inspired to the angels, "I am with you, so strengthen those who have believed. ..."}

It is also narrated in 'Sahih Al-Bukhari' and 'Sahih Muslim', in the Hadith of [Allah's] manifestation, that the Prophet (PBUH) said "... and He asks them and makes them firm ...". He (the Almighty) said to His Messenger (PBUH):

{وَكُلاًّ نَقُصُّ عَلَيْكَ مِنْ أَنْبَاءِ الرُّسُلِ مَا نُثَبِّتُ بِهِ فُؤَادَكَ ...}
[هود:120]

{And each [story] We relate to you from the news of the messengers is that by which We make firm your heart ...} [11:120]

Therefore, the people are divided into two types: the successful through the Allah's strengthening, and the forsaken through the lack of Allah's strengthening. The origin and essence of Allah's strengthening is from the firm word and following the commands; through them Allah makes firm His servant. The firmer the word and the better the deed, the greater is the strengthening by Allah. Allah (the Almighty) said:

{... وَلَوْ أَنَّهُمْ فَعَلُوا مَا يُوعَظُونَ بِهِ لَكَانَ خَيْرًا لَهُمْ وَأَشَدَّ تَثْبِيتًا}
[النساء:66]

{... But if they had done what they were instructed, it would have been better for them and a firmer position [for them in faith].} [4:66]

Those with the firmest hearts are those with the firmest words. The firm word is the truth, which is the opposite of the false lying word. There are two types of words: a firm word, which is true, and a false word, which has no truth. The firmest word is the statement of Allah's oneness and its prerequisites; it is the greatest thing with which Allah makes firm His servants in this life and the Hereafter. That is why you see the truthful among the firmest and bravest of people, and the liar among the most despised, wicked and twisted, and the least firm of people. The wise recognize the truthfulness of the truthful from his firmness of heart, his courage and his grandeur in the time of trial, and they recognize the falsehood of the liar from the opposite of that.

This is not hidden except from those of weak insight. Someone of them was asked about something he heard from someone else, so he said, "By Allah! I did not understand any of it. However, I heard in his voice authority, which is not a falsifier's authority." One is not given a greater bounty than the bounty of firm speech. People of the firm word find its fruit when they need it most, in their graves and on the day of their return, as narrated in 'Sahih Muslim' from Al-Baraa' ibn 'Azib, from the Prophet (PBUH), that this verse has been revealed concerning the torment of the grave. This has been stated clearly in a number of authentic Hadiths. They include the Hadith stated in Al-Musnad, from Dawud ibn abu Hind, from Abu Nadrah, that Abu Saied said, "We were with the Prophet (PBUH) in a funeral, and He said, "O people! The people of this Ummah are tried in their graves. When a human being is laid in his grave and his companions return, an angel comes to him with an iron hammer in his hand, makes him sit and asks him, "What do you say about this man [Muhammad (PBUH)]?" If he is a believer, he says, "I bear witness that there is no deity except Allah, alone, no partner has HE, and I bear witness that Muhammad is His slave and Messenger." Then it will be said to him,

"Correct!" Then a door is opened to Hellfire and it is said, "This would have been your place if you had disbelieved in your Lord. Since you believed, Allah has given you this place instead of it." He wants to get up to it but he is told, "Dwell," and his grave would be made spacious. As for the disbeliever or the hypocrite, when he is asked, "What do you say about this man [Muhammad (PBUH)]?" He will say, "I do not know." He is told, "Neither did you know nor did you take the guidance." Then a door is opened to Paradise and it is said, "This would have been your place if you had believed in your Lord. Since you believed, Allah has given you this place instead of it." Then the angel strikes him with the hammer between his two ears, and he will cry that will be heard by all creatures except human beings and Jinn." Some of the Companions said, "O Allah's Messenger! None of us has an angel stand over his head, with an iron hammer in his hand, except panics. The Messenger (PBUH) said, "{Allah keeps firm those who believe, with the firm word, in worldly life and in the Hereafter. And Allah sends astray the wrongdoers. And Allah does what He wills.} [14:27]""

It is also narrated in Al-Musnad from Al-Minhal, from Amr ibn Zad, from Al-Baraa' ibn 'Azib that the Messenger (PBUH) mentioned the departure of the believer's soul and said, "A visitor visits him (meaning in his grave), so he says, "Who is your Lord, what is your religion, and who is your Prophet?" He says, "My Lord is Allah, my religion is Islam, and my Prophet is Muhammad (PBUH)." He scolds him and says, "Who is your Lord, what is your religion, and who is your Prophet?" This is the last trial for the believer, and it is the situation referred to in the verse: {Allah keeps firm those who believe, with the firm word, in worldly life and in the Hereafter ...} He says, "My Lord is Allah, my religion is Islam, and my Prophet is Muhammad (PBUH)." He is told, "Correct!"" This is an authentic Hadith.

Hammad ibn Salamah conveys from Muhammad ibn Amr and from Abu Salamah, from Abu Hurairah, that the Messenger (PBUH) said, "{Allah keeps firm those who believe, with the firm word, in worldly life and in the Hereafter.}: When he is asked in the grave, "Who is your Lord and what is your religion?" He says, "My Lord is Allah, my religion is Islam, and my Prophet is Muhammad (PBUH), he came to us with clear proofs from Allah, so I believed and accepted him." He is told, "Correct! You have lived as such, you have died as such, and you shall be resurrected as such.""

Al-A'mash narrates from Al-Minhal ibn Amr, from Zadan, from Al-Baraa' ibn 'Azib that the Messenger (PBUH) mentioned the departure of the believer's soul and said, "Thereupon, his soul returns to his body, and two strong angels are sent to him, so they sit him up, scold him and say, "Who is your Lord?" So he says, "Allah." They say, "What is your religion?" So he says, "Islam." They say, "Who is this man that was sent among you?" He says, "Muhammad (PBUH); the Messenger of Allah." They say to him, "How do you know that?" He says, "I recited the book of Allah, so I believed and accepted."" He (PBUH) adds, "This is the saying of Allah (the Blessed, the Almighty): {Allah keeps firm those who believe, with the firm word, in worldly life and in the Hereafter.}" It was narrated by Ibn Hibban in his 'Sahih', and by Imam Ahmad.

He also narrated in his 'Sahih', a Hadith from Abu Hurairah, which he attributed to the Prophet (PBUH) wherein he says, "The deceased hears the footsteps of his companions turned away from him, departing. If he was a believer, Salat (Prayer) stands by his head, Zakat (Almsgiving) stands to his right, Saem (fasting) stands to his left and good deeds such as charity, maintaining the ties of kinship, and courtesy and kindness to people stand by his feet. He is approached from his head, so Salat says, "There is no entrance from here," he is approached from his right, so Zakat says, "There is no entrance from here," he is approached from his left, so fasting says, "There is no entrance from here," and he is approached from his feet, so the good deeds such as charity, maintaining the ties of kinship, and courtesy and kindness to people say, "There is no entrance from here." Then he is told, "Sit up," so he sits up, and he sun is represented for him approaching sunset. He is told, "Answer our questions." He says, "What are your questions? Leave me to pray." He is told, "You shall do so, so answer our questions." He says, "What are your questions?" They say, "Regarding that man who was sent among you, what do you say about him and what is your testimony in him?" He says, "Muhammad (PBUH)?" They say, "Yes." He says, "I testify that he is the Messenger of Allah, and that he came to us with clear proof from Allah, so we believed him." He is told, "You have lived as such, you have died as such, and you shall be resurrected as such, by Allah's will." Then his grave is extended by seventy arm-lengths and a light is provided for him therein. Then a door is opened for him to Paradise and he is told, "Look at what Allah prepared for you therein," so he becomes more happy and delighted, then his soul is placed among the good souls, in green birds suspended from the trees of Paradise, and his body is returned to the dust. That is Allah's saying: {Allah keeps firm those who believe, with the firm word, in worldly life and in the Hereafter.}"

Do not deem this parenthetical chapter too long, for the Mufti[32], the witness, the ruler and every Muslim have a stronger need for it than food, drink and breath. Success is from Allah.

---

[32] who have specialized in fiqh and issuing fatwas

Al-Hajj 22:30-31

Another analogy is the saying of Allah (the Almighty):

{... فَاجْتَنِبُوا الرِّجْسَ مِنَ الأَوْثَانِ وَاجْتَنِبُوا قَوْلَ الزُّورِ} {حُنَفَاءَ لِلَّهِ غَيْرَ مُشْرِكِينَ بِهِ وَمَنْ يُشْرِكْ بِاللَّهِ فَكَأَنَّمَا خَرَّ مِنَ السَّمَاءِ فَتَخْطَفُهُ الطَّيْرُ أَوْ تَهْوِي بِهِ الرِّيحُ فِي مَكَانٍ سَحِيقٍ} [الحج:30-31]

{... So avoid the uncleanliness of idols and avoid false statement,} {Inclining [only] to Allah, not associating [anything] with Him. And he who associates with Allah - it is as though he had fallen from the sky and was snatched by the birds or the wind carried him down into a remote place.} [22:30-31]

Observe this analogy and its accurate representation of those who associate with Allah and sought others beside him and so on. This analogy can be considered in two ways: one is to consider it a composite analogy, where the one who associates with Allah and worships others beside him is compared to a man who caused his own irrecoverable destruction, so he is compared to someone who fell from the sky and was snatched by birds and is ripped apart in their stomachs, or the wind blew him away until it carried him down into a remote location. This way, the elements of the analogy are not considered individually. The second way is to consider it a distributed analogy, where each element in one side of the analogy corresponds to an element in the other side. Thus, faith and monotheism, in their sublimity and honor, are compared to the sky, which is the place of ascent and descent; from it, one descends to the ground and to it, one ascends therefrom. He also compared the abandoner of faith and monotheism to the faller from the sky to the lowest of the low, in tightness and accumulated pains. The birds that snatch his organs and rip him apart represent the devils sent by Allah (the Exalted, the Majestic) upon him, constantly inciting him to evil, disturbing and worrying him to the places of his potential destruction. Every devil takes a piece of his faith and heart, just as every bird takes a piece of his flesh and organs. The wind, which carry him down to a remote place, represent his whims, which drive him to throw himself down in the lowest and farthest place from the sky.

CHAPTER 17

Al-Hajj 22:73

Another metaphor is the saying of Allah (the Almighty):

{يَا أَيُّهَا النَّاسُ ضُرِبَ مَثَلٌ فَاسْتَمِعُوا لَهُ إِنَّ الَّذِينَ تَدْعُونَ مِنْ دُونِ اللَّهِ لَنْ يَخْلُقُوا ذُبَابًا وَلَوِ اجْتَمَعُوا لَهُ وَإِنْ يَسْلُبْهُمُ الذُّبَابُ شَيْئًا لَا يَسْتَنْقِذُوهُ مِنْهُ ضَعُفَ الطَّالِبُ وَالْمَطْلُوبُ} [الحج:73]

{O people, an example is presented, so listen to it. Indeed, those you invoke besides Allah will never create [as much as] a fly, even if they gathered together for that purpose. And if the fly should steal away from them a [tiny] thing, they could not recover it from him. Weak are the pursuer and pursued.} [22:73]

Every servant is entitled to listen to this example, and ponder upon it duly, because it severs the cords of polytheism from his heart. Because the worshipped should at the very least be able to bring benefit to his worshipper and protect him from harm. However, these gods worshipped beside Allah by those polytheists cannot create a fly, even if they joined forces for creating it, so how about what is bigger than this [fly]? They cannot even take vengeance upon a fly if it stole something that they had of perfumes and the like; they cannot recover that from it. Thus, they are neither capable of creating a fly, which is among the weakest animals, nor capable of taking vengeance upon it and recovering what it steals from them. Thus, nothing is more helpless or weaker than these gods are, so how can a sane person approve of worshipping them beside Allah (the Almighty)? This metaphor is among the most eloquent of what Allah revealed regarding the falsehood of polytheism, the ignorance of its people, the criticism of their intellects, and the testimony that the devils manipulate them more than children play with a ball. They gave divinity, whose requirements include power over everything, encompassing all things in knowledge, independence from all creatures, to be sought for every need, removing troubles, relieving grievances and answering prayers, they gave that to pictures and statues, which do not have power over even the lowest, smallest, most humble and insignificant creation of the true Divine, even if they joined forces and cooperated for that endeavor. A stronger proof for their helplessness and the non-existence of their divinity is that if this insignificant, humble, helpless, weak creature snatched away and stole something from them and they came together to salvage that from it, they will fail to do that. Then he made equal the worshipper and the worshipped in weakness and helplessness in His saying {Weak are the pursuer and pursued.} It is said, "The pursuer is the worshipper, and the pursued is the worshipped; a helpless one clinging to a helpless one." It is also said, "It is an equation between the thief and the victim, i.e. the gods and the flies, in weakness and helplessness." According to this view, the pursuer is the false god, and the pursued is the flies for what it stole. It is also said, "The purser are the flies and the pursued are the gods, as the fly pursues them seeking to take some of what they have." The correct view is that the expression encompasses all that, because weak are the worshipper, the worshipped and the thief. Whoever puts these gods on equal footing to the Powerful, the Exalted in Might, have not appraised Allah with true appraisal, have not known Him adequately and have not glorified Him His due glorification.

CHAPTER 18

Al-Baqara 2:171

Another analogy is the saying of Allah (the Almighty):

{وَمَثَلُ الَّذِينَ كَفَرُوا كَمَثَلِ الَّذِي يَنْعِقُ بِمَا لاَ يَسْمَعُ إِلاَّ دُعَاءً وَنِدَاءً صُمٌّ بُكْمٌ عُمْيٌ فَهُمْ لاَ يَعْقِلُونَ} [البقرة:171]

{The example of those who disbelieve is like that of one who shouts at what hears nothing but calls and cries [cattle or sheep] - deaf, dumb and blind, so they do not understand.} [2:171]

This analogy contained a shouter, meaning a crier at sheep and so on, and a shouted upon, which are the animals. It is said that the shouter is the worshipper, who invokes the idol, the idol is the shouted upon, and that the state of the disbeliever in his invocation is like the state of someone who shouts upon what does not hear him. This is the view of a group including Abd Al-Rahman ibn Zaid and others. The author of 'Al-Kasshaf' and others disputed this view and said, "{but calls and cries} does not help this interpretation, because idols hear nothing, neither calls nor cries. This objection was answered in three ways: One is that 'but' is redundant, meaning that it becomes 'does not hear calls or cries', and they said that Al-Asma'y cited that in the poet's saying: "[33]حراجيج ما تنفك إلا مناخة...", which is an invalid answer because 'but' is not used redundantly.

The second answer is that the analogy is about the invocation in general, not the specifics of the invoked. The third answer is that it means: "The example of those people in their invocation of their deities, which do not understand their invocation, is that of a shepherd who shouts at his sheep and gains no benefit therefrom except that he is calling and crying." Similarly, the polytheist does not gain from his invocation and worship except the effort. It is also said that it means: "The example of the disbelievers is that of the animals which do not understand from what the shepherd says except his voice." Thus, the shepherd represents the preacher to the disbelievers, and the disbelievers are the animals, the shouted upon. Sibawayh said, "It means: Your example, O Muhammad, and the example of those who disbelieve is that of the shouter and the shouted upon." According to him, it means, "The example of the disbelievers and their preacher is that of the sheep and their shouting shepherd." You can consider it a composite analogy or a distributed analogy. If you considered it a composite analogy, then it is a comparison for the disbelievers in their lack of

---

[33] Kept in Arabic as it related to error in poem build up

comprehension and benefit to the sheep, which are shouted upon by the shepherd but understand nothing from his speech except the mere voice, which is the call and cry. If you consider it a distributed analogy, then the disbelievers are the animals, and inviting them to the [right] way and guidance is the shouting, and their perceiving the mere call and cry is like the animals who perceive the mere voice of the shouter. Allah knows best.

Al-Baqara 2:261

Another metaphor is the saying of Allah (the Almighty):

{مَثَلُ الَّذِينَ يُنفِقُونَ أَمْوَالَهُمْ فِي سَبِيلِ اللَّهِ كَمَثَلِ حَبَّةٍ أَنبَتَتْ سَبْعَ سَنَابِلَ فِي كُلِّ سُنْبُلَةٍ مِائَةُ حَبَّةٍ وَاللَّهُ يُضَاعِفُ لِمَنْ يَشَاءُ وَاللَّهُ وَاسِعٌ عَلِيمٌ} [البقرة:261]

{The example of those who spend their wealth in the way of Allah is like a seed [of grain], which grows seven spikes; in each spike is a hundred grains. And Allah multiplies [His reward] for whom He wills. And Allah is all-Encompassing and Knowing.} [2:261] [34]

He (the Exalted) compared the one who spends for His sake, whether for Jihad or all channels of beneficence to someone who planted a seed, so every seed grew seven spikes, each spike contained a hundred grain, and Allah multiplies according to the

---

[34] [Note from the Translator: Once again, only verse 261 is mentioned in the book, however the analogies stated in verses 262 to 266 are also discussed.]

spender, his faith, his dedication, his adeptness, the utility of charity, its value and its adequacy, because the reward for almsgiving varies according to the faith, dedication and clinging [to the money] in one's heart, meaning giving the money with a firm heart that accepts such spending, and a soul that tolerates it; it came out of his heart before coming out of his hand; thus, his heart is firm upon giving it, not panicked, uneasy or restless, nor are his heart and hand trembling. The reward varies according to the utility and adequacy of the spending, and according to the spender's pureness and cleverness.

One of the subtle points contained in this analogy: He (the Exalted) compared the charity to a seed. The person who spends his honestly earned fortune for the sake of Allah alone is sowing his money in a rich and fertile land. According to his seed and the fertility of his land and maintaining the seeds with irrigation and removal of foreign bushes and plants, if all these factors combined, and if the plant was not destroyed by fire or blight, it will come [on the Day of Judgment] as big as mountains, and its example will be that of a seed on a hill, which is a high ground where the seed is directly exposed to the sun and the wind, so the trees are nurtured properly, the sky rains on them abundantly and successively, watering them and causing their growth, so they yield their fruits in double because of that downpour. Even if it is not hit by a downpour, then a drizzle is sufficient due to its adequate sprout, so it grows and flourishes on that drizzle. Mentioning the two types of rain, the downpour and the drizzle, is an indication to the two types of spending: the plentiful and the scarce. The spending of some people is a downpour, and the spending of some of them is a drizzle. Allah does not allow the weight of an atom of deeds to be lost. If this person came upon what floods his work and nullifies his good deeds, he is like a man who had a garden of palm trees and grapevines underneath which rivers flow in which he has from every fruit, but he is afflicted with old age and has weak offspring, and it is hit by a whirlwind containing fire and is burned. Therefore, when the day comes for reaping the rewards and receiving the recompense, that person will find that his deeds were struck by the same calamity as the garden's owner, and his anguish then will be worse than the man's anguish over his garden. This is an analogy presented by Allah (the Exalted) regarding the torment over dispossession of the bounty in the time of dire need in addition to its great value and benefit. The person who was deprived of it was afflicted with old age and weakness, so he was in great need of such bounty. Moreover, he had weak offspring who cannot help him or run his errands; they are rather dependent on him. Thus, his need for his bounty at that time is as great as can be due to his weakness and the weakness of his offspring. If this man had a great garden that contains of all kinds of fruits and crops, and the kings of his crops are the most beautiful and beneficial of fruits, palm trees and grapevines; the palm trees suffice him and his offspring, but he woke up one day and found it all burned as though reaped, so what sorrow is greater than his? Ibn Abbas said, "This is a metaphor for one who ends his life with corruption." Mujahid said, "This is an example for one who neglects the obedience of Allah until he dies." Al-Suddy said, "This is an analogy for the one who spends only to be seen by people, who spends for the sake of someone other than Allah, so he is deprived of its benefit when he needs it most." Umar ibn Al-Khattab asked the Companions (may Allah be pleased with them) one day about this verse, so they said, "Allah knows best," so Umar got angry and said, "Say either 'We know,' or 'We do not know'." Ibn Abbas said, "There is something in my heart regarding that verse, O Amir Al-Mu'minin " He said, "Say it, my nephew, and do not keep it to yourself." He said, "It is an analogy given for a deed." He said, "What deed?" He said, "A wealthy man who does good deeds, then Allah sent Satan upon him, so he did evil deeds until he burned all his deeds." Al-Hassan said, "This is an analogy that few people, to my knowledge, understand. An old man with a weak body and many children, his need for his garden is the highest it has ever been, and, indeed, each of you is most in need for his deeds when he departs from the worldly life."

If these deeds of charity are exposed to what nullifies them such as reminders [of favor], hurt and pretension. Pretention prevents the reward that results from charity, while reminders and hurt abolish the reward that resulted from it. The example of it is like that of a large smooth stone upon which is dust and is hit by a downpour that leaves it bare, with nothing on it. Look closely at the elements of this eloquent metaphor and their accurate representation in order to understand the greatness and sublimity of the Holy Qur'an. The stone corresponds to the heart of the pretentious, reminder and hurtful person. His heart, in its hardness against faith, dedication and kindness, is like the stone. The deed that is performed for the sake of someone other than Allah is like the dust on that stone. The hardness of what is beneath it prevent it from stability and growth upon the pouring of the rain. It has no substance to connect it to what accepts the water and brings forth grass. Similarly, the pretentious person's heart has no stability upon the downpour of commands, prohibitions, fate and destiny. When the downpour of revelation comes upon it, that little dust is washed away, revealing what is beneath it as a hard stone without any plants therein. This is a metaphor presented by Allah for the deeds and charity of the pretentious person, who cannot attain, on the Day of Judgment, any reward therefor, when he needs it most. Success is from Allah.

Another analogy is the saying of Allah (the Almighty):

{إِنَّ الَّذِينَ كَفَرُوا لَنْ تُغْنِيَ عَنْهُمْ أَمْوَالُهُمْ وَلَا أَوْلَادُهُمْ مِنَ اللَّهِ شَيْئًا وَأُولَئِكَ أَصْحَابُ النَّارِ هُمْ فِيهَا خَالِدُونَ} {مَثَلُ مَا يُنْفِقُونَ فِي هَذِهِ الْحَيَاةِ الدُّنْيَا كَمَثَلِ رِيحٍ فِيهَا صِرٌّ أَصَابَتْ حَرْثَ قَوْمٍ ظَلَمُوا أَنْفُسَهُمْ فَأَهْلَكَتْهُ وَمَا ظَلَمَهُمُ اللَّهُ وَلَكِنْ أَنْفُسَهُمْ يَظْلِمُونَ} [آل عمران:116-117]

{Indeed, those who disbelieve - never will their wealth or their children avail them against Allah at all, and those are the companions of the Fire; they will abide therein eternally.} {The example of what they spend in this worldly life is like that of a wind containing frost which strikes the harvest of a people who have wronged themselves and destroys it. And Allah has not wronged them, but they wrong themselves.} [3:116-117]

This metaphor is given by Allah (the Almighty) for those who spend their wealth in a way that disobeys and displeases him. He (the Exalted) compared what those people spend out of nobility pride and seeking praise and respect, and not for the sake of Allah, as well as what they spend to avert people from the way of Allah and His Messengers (PBUT), He compared that with the plant sowed by its farmer seeking its benefit and good, but it was struck by very cold wind, the coldness of which burns the plants and crops it passes by, so it destroyed this harvest and dried it out. The meaning of the word 'الصر' [translated here as frost' is debated. Some say it means 'intense cold', some say it means 'fire', which is the view of Ibn Abbas. Ibn Al-Anbary said, "Fire was called that due to '…' in its blaze." It is also said, "It means the sound that accompanies the strong wind." The three views are related; it is an intense cold that burns the crops due because of its drought, and it is accompanied by a loud sound. His saying {… which strikes the harvest of a people who have wronged themselves …} includes a warning that the reason for its striking is their wrongdoing. He is the one who sent this aforementioned wind upon them until it destroyed their plants and dried it out. Their wrongdoing is the wind that destroyed and spoiled their deeds and expenditures.

Az-Zumar 39:29

Another metaphor is the saying of Allah (the Almighty):

{ضَرَبَ اللّهُ مَثَلاً رَجُلاً فِيهِ شُرَكَاءُ مُتَشَاكِسُونَ وَرَجُلاً سَلَمًا لِرَجُلٍ هَلْ يَسْتَوِيَانِ مَثَلاً الْحَمْدُ لِلّهِ بَلْ أَكْثَرُهُمْ لاَ يَعْلَمُونَ} [الزمر:29]

{Allah presents an example: a slave owned by quarreling partners and another belonging exclusively to one man; are they equal in comparison? Praise be to Allah! But most of them do not know.} [39:29]

This is an example presented by Allah for the polytheist and the monotheist. The polytheist is like a slave owned by a group of people who jointly own his service, but he cannot please all of them at the same time, and the monotheist, since he worships Allah alone, he is like a slave owned exclusively by one man, the desire of whom he knew his desire and the path to whose satisfaction he understood. Therefore, he is free from the quarrelling of partners in his ownership, for he is devoted to his owner without an adversary, in addition to the mercy, kindness and compassion of his owner towards him and his looking out for his best interests; are these two slaves on equal footing? This is a very eloquent example, because the slave that is exclusive to one owner attains of his aid, kindness, attention and undertaking of his interests what cannot be attained by the slave jointly owned by the quarrelling owners. {Praise be to Allah! But most of them do not know.}

At-Tahrim 66:10-12

Another analogy is the saying of Allah (the Almighty):

{ضَرَبَ اللّهُ مَثَلاً لِلّذِينَ كَفَرُوا امْرَأَتَ نُوحٍ وَامْرَأَتَ لُوطٍ كَانَتَا تَحْتَ عَبْدَيْنِ مِنْ عِبَادِنَا صَالِحَيْنِ فَخَانَتَاهُمَا فَلَمْ يُغْنِيَا عَنْهُمَا مِنَ اللّهِ شَيْئًا وَقِيلَ ادْخُلَا النَّارَ مَعَ الدَّاخِلِينَ} {وَضَرَبَ اللّهُ مَثَلاً لِلّذِينَ آمَنُوا امْرَأَتَ فِرْعَوْنَ إِذْ قَالَتْ رَبِّ ابْنِ لِي عِنْدَكَ بَيْتًا فِي الْجَنَّةِ وَنَجِّنِي مِنْ فِرْعَوْنَ وَعَمَلِهِ وَنَجِّنِي مِنَ الْقَوْمِ الظَّالِمِينَ} {وَمَرْيَمَ ابْنَتَ عِمْرَانَ الَّتِي أَحْصَنَتْ فَرْجَهَا فَنَفَخْنَا فِيهِ مِنْ رُوحِنَا وَصَدَّقَتْ بِكَلِمَاتِ رَبِّهَا وَكُتُبِهِ وَكَانَتْ مِنَ الْقَانِتِينَ} [التحريم:10-12]

{Allah presents an example of those who disbelieved: the wife of Noah and the wife of Lot. They were under two of Our righteous servants but betrayed them, so those prophets did not avail them from Allah at all, and it was said, "Enter the Fire with those who enter."} {And Allah presents an example of those who believed: the wife of Pharaoh, when she said, "My Lord, build for me near You a house in Paradise and save me from Pharaoh and his deeds and save me from the wrongdoing people."} {And [the example of] Mary, the daughter of 'Imran, who guarded her chastity, so

We blew into [her garment] through Our angel, and she believed in the words of her Lord and His scriptures and was of the devoutly obedient.} [66:10-12]

These verses contained three examples: one for the disbelievers and one for the believers. The disbelievers' example included that the disbeliever is reprimanded for his disbelief and animosity towards Allah (the Almighty), His Messengers and His allies. It does not avail him, in the presence of his disbelief, whatever blood, marital or any other relations to the believers. All these reasons are severed on the Day of Judgment except what is connected to Allah, alone, at the hands of His Messengers (PBUH). If the ties of kinship or marriage could avail with the lack of faith, the relations between Noah, Lot (PBUT) and their respective wives would have availed them, but they did not avail them from Allah at all, and they were told, "Enter Hellfire with those who enter." Therefore, the verse cut the hopes of those who disobeyed Allah, went against His commands and wished that the righteousness of a relative or a stranger would benefit him, even if they had the strongest relation in this life. There is no stronger tie than the ties of prophethood, parenthood and marriage. However, Noah (PBUH) did not avail his son, Abraham (PBUH) did not avail his father, and Noah and Lot (PBUT) did not avail their wives from Allah at all. Allah (the Almighty) said:

{لَنْ تَنْفَعَكُمْ أَرْحَامُكُمْ وَلَا أَوْلَادُكُمْ يَوْمَ الْقِيَامَةِ يَفْصِلُ بَيْنَكُمْ ...}
[الممتحنة:3]

{Never will your relatives or your children benefit you; the Day of Resurrection He will judge between you ...} [60:3]

He (the Almighty) also said:

{يَوْمَ لاَ تَمْلِكُ نَفْسٌ لِنَفْسٍ شَيْئًا وَالأَمْرُ يَوْمَئِذٍ لِلَّهِ} [الانفطار:19]

{It is the Day when a soul will not possess for another soul [power to do] a thing; and the command, that Day, is [entirely] with Allah.} [82:19]

He (the Almighty) also said:

{وَاتَّقُوا يَوْمًا لاَ تَجْزِي نَفْسٌ عَنْ نَفْسٍ شَيْئًا ...} [البقرة:48/123]

{And fear a Day when no soul will suffice for another soul at all ...} [2:48/123]

He (the Almighty) also said:

{... وَاخْشَوْا يَوْمًا لاَ يَجْزِي وَالِدٌ عَنْ وَلَدِهِ وَلاَ مَوْلُودٌ هُوَ جَازٍ عَنْ وَالِدِهِ شَيْئًا ...} [لقمان:31]

{... and fear a Day when no father will avail his son, nor will a son avail his father at all ...} [31:33]

All this is to deny the false hopes of the disbelievers that what they put their trust in, such as kinship, marriage or friendship, will avail them on the Day of Judgment, protect them from the punishment of Allah (the Almighty) or intercede with Allah on their behalf. This is the root of the humanity's corruption and polytheism, it is the association [with Allah], which Allah does not forgive, it is what Allah (the Almighty) sent all His Messengers (PBUT) and revealed all His Books to nullify and to wage war and declare hostility against its people.

As for the two believers' examples, one of them is the wife of Pharaoh. The similarity is that the believer's tie to the disbeliever does not harm him if he separated himself from him in his disbelief and deeds. The sins of the disobedient does not harm the obedient in the Hereafter, even if it harmed him in the worldly life, because of the punishment that befalls the people of the Earth if they abandon the commands of Allah, such punishment comes unexclusively. The wife of Pharaoh was not harmed by her connection to him, despite him being of the most disbelieving disbelievers, just as the wives of Noah and Lot (PBUT) were not availed by their connection to them, despite them being the Messengers of the Lord of the worlds.

The second example for the believers is Mary, who had no husband, whether a believer or a disbeliever. Thus, Allah mentioned the three types of women: the disbelieving woman who is tied to a righteous man, the righteous woman who is tied to a disbelieving man, and the single woman who has no ties to anyone. The first is not availed by her tie or its cause, the second is not harmed by her tie or its cause, and the third is not harmed by her lack of ties at all. These examples contain subtle points that fit the context of the Surat [chapter], because it came in the context of mentioning the wives of the Prophet (PBUH) and warning of cooperating against him and that if they did not obey Allah and His Messenger (PBUH) and did not desire the Hereafter, their relation to the Messenger (PBUH) will not avail them, just as such relation did not avail the wives of Noah and Lot (PBUT). That is why He gave them, in this Surat, the examples of the ties of marriage and not the ties of kinship.

Yahia ibn Salam said, "Allah gave the first example to warn Aisha and Hafsah (may Allah be pleased with them), then he gave them the second example to encourage them to adhere to obedience." Giving the example of Mary has another consideration: She was not harmed, in Allah's perspective, at all by the Jews', the enemies of Allah, accusations of her and charging her and her son with what Allah cleared them from, as she became the greatest woman of truth, chosen above the women of the world. Thus, the righteous man is not harmed by the wicked and the lewd people's accusations of him. This is to relieve Aisha (Umm Al-Mu'minin) if this Surat was revealed after the incident of Ifk[35] , or to prepare her for what the liars would say if it was revealed before the incident. The examples of the wives of Noah and Lot (PBUT) also contained a warning for her and Hafsah of what they did concerning the Prophet (PBUH). Therefore, these examples included warning and alarming for them, encouraging them to obedience and monotheism as well as relief and preparation for those who were harmed and falsely accused among them. The secrets of the revelation are much more and much greater than this, particularly the secrets of analogies, which are only understood by those of knowledge.

This is completed by the praise of Allah and his good support. May Allah bestow His blessing and complete peace on

---

[35] The incident of Ifk (falsehood) is an incident where Aisha (may Allah be pleased with her) was falsely accused of committing adultery by a group of hypocrites led by Abdullah ibn Ubay, but the Qur'an exonerated her. The incident is narrated in Surat Al-Nur (The 24th Surat of the Holy Qur'an)

Muhammad, his family and his companions. May Allah forgive its writer, reader, considerer and author as well as All Muslims and believers, whether men or women. All praise is due to Allah, the Lord of the worlds.

Written by the one in need for his Lord (the Almighty), Ali ibn Zaid, may Allah forgive him, his parents and all Muslims.

All praise is due to Allah, with whose bounty good deeds are completed.

ABOUT THE AUTHOR

Imam Ibn Qayyim Al-Jawziyya (1292–1350 CE / 691 AH–751 AH)

He was born in Damascus in 691H most scholars of the time have acknowledged the author's excellence, and profound knowledge of Quranic interpretation, commentaries on the prophetic traditions, and theology. His extensive knowledge and understanding of Quranic commentaries surpassed even some renowned theologians in Islamic history.

He is the most outstanding student of Shaikh-ul-Islaam Ibn Taimiyyah, may Allah have mercy on all of them. And work hard on protecting his teacher writings and save them.

After Ibn Taimiyyah dead he starts teaching, and he has many students who became famous Scholars Example Ibn Rajab.

.

www.ingramcontent.com/pod-product-compliance
Lightning Source LLC
Chambersburg PA
CBHW020238030726
47497CB00009B/3154